LOSING EUGENIO

LOSING EUGENIO

A novel by
Geneviève Brisac

translated from the French by
J.A. Underwood

MARION BOYARS
LONDON • NEW YORK

Published in Great Britain and the United States
in 1999 by Marion Boyars Publishers
24 Lacy Road London SW15 1NL
237 East 39th Street New York NY 10016

Published in 1999
10 9 8 7 6 5 4 3 2 1

Originally published in 1996 by Éditions de l'Olivier/Le Seuil, Paris,
under the title *Week-end de chasse à la mère*
© by Éditions de l'Olivier/Le Seuil, 1996
© This translation J.A. Underwood
All rights reserved.

British Library Cataloguing in Publication Data.
A catalogue record for this book is available from the British Library.

A CIP catalog record for this book is available from the Library of Congress.

ISBN 0-7145-3049-2 Paperback

Typeset in 11½/14pt Caslon by Ann Buchan (Typesetters), Middlesex
Printed in Great Britain by WPC Book Manufacturers
Bridgend, Mid Glamorgan

This book has been published with financial assistance
from the Arts Council of Great Britain

1

'What's your favourite animal?' Eugenio asked as we walked home that night. It was two days to Christmas.

I said: 'Koala bear, squirrel, otter. Koala bear, for the way it puts its paws round the trunk of the eucalyptus tree and for being related to the kangaroo. Squirrel, for the nuts. Such sweetness in the giving of a nut, I always say. Otter, I'm not sure. Because of the touchingly ugly sound of its name. Because of water.'

I was lying. I had in mind more of an armadillo type of creature.

Eugenio had slipped his arm into the little invisible handle formed by my body and my arm. He sounded bothered:

'Do you think Queen Elizabeth has had a happy life?' he asked in a quiet voice.

I had a mean retort on the tip of my tongue: Who's been talking to you about that stuffed dummy in a hat? It's your father again, isn't it, he's been talking to you about her!

What I said was: 'Fairly happy, I think, but she's been let down by her children.'

It was a piece of gratuitous spite, uttering those words in the same breath: *let down* and *children*. Eugenio flinched.

I felt ashamed.

'Better get your skates on,' Eugenio said then. 'We're late, mummy, get your skates on!'

'That is a truly awful expression and one Queen Elizabeth would certainly never use,' I replied.

Queen Elizabeth is our idol, Aunt Sally, sphinx and scapegoat combined.

'She hasn't had a happy life,' I said eventually, 'because she's never particularly looked for one.'

Such dignity made him thoughtful. I was reminded, one thing leading to another, of a different queen, whose knicker elastic gave and who died as a result, died of cold in the snow because she refused to get up from the stone bench where she had salvaged her threatened dignity. I told Eugenio the story: dying of cold on an icy stone bench is the height of dignity, I pointed out, suddenly proud of my little educational sortie. But Eugenio sniggered: 'Blinded by romanticism yet again, mummy. It wasn't like that at all. The queen screamed and raged, ten men were sent for, among the strongest in the kingdom, and they ripped out the stone bench and carried it into the palace, sweating and puffing like anything, so that no one, ever, would be able to whisper: the queen lost her knickers. That, if you like, is the height of dignity.'

Eugenio is more in touch with the royal mind than I am.

I took out my key on its Marge Simpson key-ring. Marge Simpson, so sweet with her everlasting blue hair-do. In the foyer of the building, birdsong became audible, trilling birdsong.

The whole stairwell rang with their vocal exercises, because they lived at the bottom of the stairs, where the pushchairs are usually parked. Every time we passed their great big cage with its confusing arabesques, something made me say: 'Listen, Eugenio, the angels are singing.' And every time, his twitch of irritation reprimanded me. Just as I would say to him every morning on the way to school: 'Look at that house, it's the best house in all Paris. It's very white, very smooth, with a little garden at the side and gravel paths and little clumps of roses half-hidden behind impenetrable green railings. It has such tall windows, one imagines a face with a massive forehead and oblong eyes.'

Eugenio would answer: 'You say the same thing over and over again: look, listen, look, listen …'

'Leave my eyes and ears alone,' he said seriously.

As we climbed the stairs, me in front and him behind, clinging to my skirts, a hangover from the time (not all that long ago) when I used to carry him up, in defiance of every recommendation, cocking a snook at the entire medical profession, through sheer stupidity, I remembered what he'd been saying a moment before: 'Get your skates on mummy, we're late.'

'Who are we late for?' I asked suspiciously, and he laughed.

'That was just a trick to make you go faster,' he muttered, a little unnerved by his own insolence. 'You're always saying there's no education but by example. "We're late" are the two words you say most often.' He mimicked the face I make, neck tensed, jaws clenched, brow furrowed with anxiety: '"We're late, hurry up darling!"'

'But I don't do that when it's holidays!'

'I do,' Eugenio answered. 'Look, it's nearly Christmas, mummy.

We really do have to get our skates on. Where are we going, anyway, we're not staying here, are we, getting on each other's nerves? Other people have families they love, what's to become of us?'

'While we're on the subject, what are we going to eat?' I asked.

A clear voice from the depths of the sofa suggested: 'McDonald's?'

'A McDonald's that I go out and fetch you, or a McDonald's that we eat there, like lovers?' My grounded poet hesitated, startled by such indulgence.

'That you go out and fetch,' he concluded after mature reflection. And I felt a pang of anguish. 'All right, love. What kind of McDonald's?'

Before going out again, I drew the curtains that I had eventually put up in our living-room, blood-red, heavy curtains, extremely formal. They reminded me of when I had worked in the theatre, that was what they were there for, to remind me of worlds I had resigned from. I looked down at the narrow street. The dark winter night is different for every window, I mused. In the one-and-a-half rooms where Eugenio and I had been living for two years, there were two. Directly opposite, let into the opposite wall, there was a plaque I had never noticed before, a sort of little scene, green, lit by a tiny spotlight. It seemed to show a landscape, boulders probably, and a lake. It was hard to make out anything but silvery reflections. I was reminded of Ys, the magical Breton city that only comes up out of the water once in a hundred years.

The McDonald's in the boulevard was half-empty. On the left as you came in, just inside the door, sat Violet. That was my name for her, anyway, because she was a woman at peace. Violet would tell me things from time to time, it was why she came there, to have a chat with someone. She would carry over her orange plastic box containing some mess she had concocted herself, using other people's debris. I never asked her what she was eating, we talked about our children, about life. That evening she had finished her meal and was clearing things away, muttering to herself. She picked up about twenty drinking-straws and stuffed them into her large bag, where they joined the empty plastic bags that rustled as she walked. The existence of Violet, far from distressing me, reassured me. Why? Because of her graceful movements, I think, and because she was not sad, despite the fact that she was old, poor and on her own.

Farther down the spacious interior full of orange reflections, half-hidden behind the central pillar, I spotted the thoughtful, happy face of the tramp who used to spend the day begging just up the street. He virtually lived in the restaurant. He slept there, ate there twice a day, always at the same time, using the same table. He was a resident, he would fasten his paper serviette around his neck.

I took the order back up to my son, together with a large fries, Chinese sauce and a straw.
    'Put it down at my feet, slave,' he said.

I had not even taken off my coat. I couldn't help the tears that stung my eyes at that moment. I wasn't proud of them either, any more than I was of the smack that then landed on the spiky top of his head. The fries went flying.

'You always spoil things!' I shouted.

'It was just a joke, mummy,' he spluttered. 'You have no sense of humour, you really don't. You're only thinking of yourself when you claim to be thinking of everybody. It doesn't work, and that's why you're on your own, why we're both here, the two of us, like a couple of dead rats.'

I wanted to go over to him, put my hand on his arm. I thought of those mothers whose children hit them, making people mutter: 'Serves them right. You spoil children like that, you turn them into monsters.'

'If you don't spoil them,' another voice whispered, 'you turn them into cripples.'

Eugenio did not hit me, he snuggled up to me. I sensed he was crying. We watched a quiz show: *Saved by the Bell*.

'Don't worry about Christmas,' I murmured to him, 'I've got it all planned, it's a surprise, you'll like it.'

I said this as I turned out the light. I stayed to watch him fall asleep. Never do that, the doctor would tell me every time.

Only dead mothers, I sometimes caught myself thinking, do no harm. They are the kindest ones, the really perfect ones.

The truth is, I watched my son fall asleep for the beauty of that silent moment, that split second when everything tips over. I watched him fall asleep. I took the time, the way I take time out to gaze at flowers. I just did it, trying to understand.

Only two days to Christmas Eve, I jingled in amazement as I fell asleep myself. How shall we get through it this time?

When we woke up next morning there was not a sound outside, the street was deserted, maybe the whole city.

'Buy me some birds,' Eugenio muttered as he stirred something horrible in his bowl.

'But there are the canaries in the stairwell,' I replied.

'Birds of my own, that I'd look after and that would have names,' he argued. 'Anyway, the birds in the stairwell have gone all quiet. I bet they died of cold in the night.'

Such bad faith, coupled with such callousness, made me smile.

'Go on, buy me a bird,' he said again, galvanized by his breakfast cereal and by the truce he could read on my face. And out we went.

'It's the shortest, nastiest, coldest day in the world,' Eugenio said with obvious satisfaction. 'And where are we going to spend Christmas Eve, eh, Clever-clogs? It's tomorrow now, and I can see you haven't the slightest idea where we might go. No one's expecting us, no presents, no Father Christmas for poor Eugenio. Mummy, why did you get divorced?'

He probably didn't say the last bit. Not really. It was me hearing it. Like a refrain, a beastly little refrain that went everywhere with us.

We were walking with our heads well down because of the gusts of wind at each street corner. In the Rue Dauphine, down

near the river, Eugenio saw a toyshop, and we went in. It was
more of a dark passage than a shop. I imagined the smell of
wood, varnish, amber and England that permeates such places.
I had always thought, half-consciously, that toyshops were
antechambers of other worlds and that toys were signs, clues,
even actual illusions. Without meaning to, without even realizing I was doing it, I had passed this mini-religion on to my
child. Our altars were the window displays that the big stores
put on as early as six weeks before Christmas. The dancing
teddy bears that cook blueberry tarts in tiny gilded stoves as a
throng of lady rabbits in pale-blue or yellow chiffon dresses
polka round them, waving little bouquets, all to a background
of Christmas music: these were the minor deities of our harmless liturgy.

The smell of the shop in the Rue Dauphine was full of promise.
By that I mean it was a reassuring blend of smells: dust, polish,
cake crumbs, varnished wood, old wallpaper, ink and honey,
and I cherished the hope that here was the gateway to the
world, as I dubbed it secretly. At the desk, a woman was
speaking into a mobile phone, discussing the Christmas Eve
menu. Eugenio sat on the floor, weighing up coloured-glass
eggs, unwrapping packs of tarot cards, operating cardboard
puppets with jointed limbs, his hands full of coloured balls that
had all sorts of uses, balls and cards being the mainstays of the
games industry.
    'No,' I said to Eugenio, 'there's no room at our place. We've
already got the pin-ball machine, the tortoises, the papier-
mâché fort with moats and covered way, the Lego palace of

Harun al-Rashid, the clockwork elephant that smokes a pipe, our child-sized King Kong, the dwarf ping-pong set and about seven thousand other essentials. Let's wait till things improve a bit. Where we're going to put your birds is already a problem, and we haven't even bought them yet.'

My voice had risen in pitch. The woman, sensing that we belonged to that dreadful breed who think they can do what they like, even play with items that are for sale or make a rumpus in a toyshop, put down the phone. Genuinely terrified, we fled from the shop like frightened sparrows.

'Did you hear what she was saying to her mother, the way she was talking to her?' I asked my son, to put a little dignity on our flight.

He looked at me with fathomless scorn: 'How can you possibly know it was her mother? When I write my memoirs they'll be called *My Mother was a Gossipmonger*!' he pronounced darkly.

'Oh good, you've got the title, then,' I retorted.

I told him the story of Charlie Chaplin's mother. We were walking along again, holding each other close. There was no one about. We were crossing the bridge as I told him the story. As a result, I forgot to urge him to contemplate the grey water and observe the dead tree opposite, standing in isolation on the lower embankment.

'They lived in London,' I explained. 'We don't know where the father was. It was a very run-down part of the city. There was real poverty. But Charlie's mother was no ordinary woman.

She used to stand by the window and read him the street like a narrative, everything that was happening in the street, what was going through the minds of the people, their secrets, their music. She'd say: "See that man down there, yes him, with one foot in the gutter, don't you wonder what he's doing there, why he's out in the cold? You want to know why? Well, his wife has thrown him out, without his tea even, oh they're too sad for a child, stories like that, she's thrown him out, and quite right too. He's fed up, he's hungry, you'll see, yes look, he's going into the baker's to buy a bun." And the man would come out with a bun, not a pastry, a bun. Charlie Chaplin's mother knew such things, she was a bit mad, she had some nervous trouble. They put her in a home in the end, or maybe a hospital, but she knew how to observe things and she passed the gift on to her son, she taught him to use his eyes.'

'The thing that amazes me,' Eugenio said, 'is how they never used to have croissants in England.'

He looked sad. Having his red nose and his eyes sunk deep into his face by the cold hardly helped. We were on our way to buy birds, everything should have been perfect, a moment of perfect happiness, a mother and her son, the day before Christmas Eve. I hesitated to ask Eugenio what made him so glum, I hesitated to tackle him. I thought of the first seconds of his life on earth. Why have you not got a bigger mouth, baby? That was what went through my mind as they dangled him upside-down in front of my face, which I was aware was still drawn with pain. I had always supposed that a person's chance of happiness increased with the size of his or her mouth, and my new baby was certainly not blessed. A tiny, improbably tiny cherry. Perhaps that was why, immediately, I loved him too much. Perhaps that was why his secret name became Liubov, which, as everyone knows, means *love*.

2

The Place du Châtelet was empty and the embankment deserted. 'I'm very much afraid the bird shop's going to be closed,' I told Eugenio. It was eleven in the morning.

We were walking amid half-frozen fig trees and an army of firs of all sizes rather like human beings, striking in their diversity.

'How does one choose?' Eugenio murmured.

'Choose what?' I replied in an equally low voice.

'Animals, of course!'

I liked that, the way he referred to birds as 'animals'.

I said: 'What really matters is choosing the right shop.'

They were all the same. Still, we did not enter the first one (a tourist trap), nor the second (too dirty), nor the one after, which had heavy wire mesh across it and where you could hear animals whining in the back. Then we had to hurry past a dark passage because it smelled of hyena. (Everyone will know what I mean, which is rough on hyenas, we all know how awful they are, how they stink, whereas giraffes, which are universally adored, stink even more and are no better.)

We went into Papageno's. That was the name of the shop: 'Papageno, bird-catcher, nurseryman, pets of all descriptions.'

Papagena approached. She was a red-headed giantess, with short hairs plastered against her forehead, a woolly hat, rubber boots that had once been white, a chestnut cardigan textured like a heavy-duty floorcloth, huge strangler's hands with spatulate fingers and a white coat like a butcher. Eugenio asked to see the canaries.

We had to walk past dozens of empty cages.

The ones I liked best were the exotic cages resembling mosques. Some were the size of a room. I felt there had just been some sort of exodus. In my mind's eye the perches still swung slightly. Eugenio was tugging at my hand, clearly worried. 'Stop pulling,' I grumbled. And I decided not to draw his attention to the dead pigeon lying in a corner. I also decided provisionally against inviting him to shed a pious tear over 'our' pigeon, the one that had come to die on our balcony the previous summer as if he had sought out our company, impressing Eugenio with his air of weariness and gloom, his dying-pigeon breathing, his little stiff legs in the morning when we found him lying on his back ... That's enough, I thought.

Nor did I say anything to him about the slightly alarming seagull pacing to and fro like a doorman, the way seagulls do sometimes.

The back part of the shop was more crowded because of the puppies.

'Can I pick one up?' my son pleaded. As any child would have done, I imagined.

My reply was hesitant: 'I'm sure it's not allowed.'

'Oh all right,' I added, swept off my feet by a desire to defy the law, 'we'll say we're thinking of buying one.'

Eugenio had a go with all the little dogs, monitored fiercely by one of Papageno's minions. He fell in love with a spaniel pup, a poodle and a third, unidentifiable bundle of fur. 'We must rescue them all,' he kept telling me, 'just think what sort of childhood they're having!'

'They are dogs, don't forget,' I said.

I spared him the lament of those who would prefer that a trickle-down sentimentalism did not wash over us endlessly, mixing up humans with baby seals, the mute pain of the boiled crab with the tragedy of the Tutsis.

What I said was: 'We'll come back at night and open their cages, darling.'

He said: 'It's a deal.'

And with a smile that was my recompense for many things, he turned to the saleslady: 'We've decided, we'll take two canaries.'

Papagena came hurrying up: 'Two canaries, two!'

'A male and a female,' Eugenio slipped in, 'isn't that right, mummy? We want them to be happy. As happy as the canaries in the stairwell. Maybe they'll make friends?' Clearly it was in the hope of seeing his horrid little creatures lay eggs that Eugenio talked of them being happy. I said: 'Next stop a full aviary, thousands of canaries in every conceivable colour, feathers all silken, a heavenly cantilena of canaries. I'll sell the hi-fi, we'll listen to our birds. Apparently they have to sing with their beaks closed. Some even die, they strive so.'

'I'm sorry but I think you're getting confused with swans,' Eugenio said, pained by my lyricism.

Adam and Eve, our canaries-to-be. Adam, the larger one, Eve the smaller — according to the saleslady, that is, and it seemed logical to us, though both had immaculate white plumage, with yellow beaks impeccably closed and anyway they were wrapped now, each in its little plastic cloche. We still needed the cage and the bits and pieces.

'They're having a happy Christmas, at any rate,' Eugenio stated with satisfaction. 'Pity we can't rescue more.'

'It's called buying, not rescuing!' I pointed out, pulling him towards the accessories section. The banks of cages were like blocks of flats. Hard to tell who is copying whom any more, I thought to myself. The same perch, the same seed tray, endlessly repeated. We chose a size two.

'There may well be prettier ones at the flea market,' I said loudly to annoy the saleslady. 'Real Arabian Nights cages with gilded onion domes and masses of swings and decorative friezes, I've seen one at my cousin's. It would be like being caught up in a dream, our birds would think they were nightingales.'

'These cages are disinfected every Friday,' she said crossly.

'Is she deaf, do you think, or just stupid?' my son whispered.

There was a lot to carry, I realized: Adam's cloche in one hand and Eve's in the other, the cage in a twist of rather smelly newspaper clutched in Eugenio's arms, the various seeds and the little toy to help them get used to their new life still lying on top of the till. I wrote out a cheque, suddenly impatient to have done with it all.

'I'm hungry,' said Eugenio.

I was prevented from clouting him by my many packages, and we left the shop in silence. Some of the nicest outings end like that. In disappointment, bitterness and the back of a taxi.

Eugenio was glued to the off-side window, drawing rabbits in the condensation. I sat stiffly at the far end of the seat, the cage on my knees. Adam and Eve chirped on the floor, clearly delighted by their blindfold journey. The driver must have found the human silence heavy and the bird noise irritating.

'Well, old man, what are you getting for Christmas?'

'I am not an old man,' my son growled uncompromisingly.

'Have you been driving a taxi long?' I asked, or something equally ridiculous. I thought I detected a sly chuckle to my left. I felt uncomfortable.

The driver seized the opportunity to start telling me his life story. Thirty years at the wheel. '... came across some treasure recently,' I heard him saying. I struggled to recall how he had reached that point. Eugenio sat slumped against me, broken-necked, another treasure, also important, I sensed, but at the same time quite natural.

'It's because I do house-moving, see?' the driver went on, studying me in his mirror. This optical arrangement seemed to slow the words down, making them bounce differently. And I returned his focused gaze directly. It is a variant of the analysis situation, I often think, when taxi-drivers reel off their litany of misfortunes for my benefit. Apparently Donald Winnicott used to debate with clerics the possible difference between treatment and confession. 'When you get bored, it's treatment,' Winnicott would explain to the priest.

'Me and some mates,' the driver was saying, wrapped up in his story, 'we have this little van. The move I'm talking about was special, though. A customer I've been ferrying about for years now, all over the country we go, Paris-Châteauroux, Paris-Limoges, Paris-Concarneau, we've had some wicked times together. Well, when he had to get out of his place, he came to me, see? "It'll be like writing yourself into my will". That's what he said, real one-foot-in-the-grave stuff.'

I warmed to the taxi-driver, I liked his style. He glanced in the mirror to make sure I was following the story.

'The owners had said to take away the furniture, take away the paintings, whatever was labelled, the valuable stuff. Anything left we could have, see? Major clear-out. All we knew was, there was some wine. Picture it: rows and rows of Romanée Conti, Pommard, Sauternes, Lachryma Christi, you name it.'

A nicer form of name-dropping, I thought: label-dropping. But even that can be overdone ... Eugenio, bored stiff by the conversation, was snoring rudely.

'The cellar was even better than we'd imagined, hundreds of bottles, all covered in dust, filling racks hundreds of feet long.'

A sudden sense of propriety, the sort you experience at the idea of overhearing stories clearly not meant for your ears, made me think of owning up to almost never drinking wine myself. As one might feel obliged to declare oneself an agnostic, or illiterate, or a foreigner. But that would have spoiled the taxi-driver's story, and anyway it was too late.

'So up we came again, carrying as many bottles as we could, we sat down at the table, we poured wine into the mugs we'd brought for our snack. And we all spat it out again. As one man. It was awful. Vintage vinegar. We quickly opened the Romanée Conti. Ever drunk a bottle of that?'

'No, never,' I said, captivated.

'A lovely wine. But again: vinegar. Every single bottle. We'd been well and truly had. Except I find it hard to believe they knew and didn't tell us. But the best thing —'

He threw me one of those storyteller's glances in the mirror, calling me to order. I had been struggling to think what had made him believe in such a huge gift in the first place.

'Underneath the bottles we felt something funny, I dug it up, it was like a little casket, the lock was all rusty and full of earth, we had to force it. Next minute, we're shaking like leaves,'

'And?' I prompted. It was the big moment. I was braced to see maggots leap out in the narrator's face, I was set to quake over hirsute spiders imported from the tropics.

'D'you like gold' he asked in a sibylline whisper.

'Yes.' Lamentable as repartee, I was aware, but I had never really seen any.

'Well, that's what it was. A pile of gold coins. And if you like gold, I can tell you, the sight does more for you than a bare-assed eighteen-year-old in your bed. Gold is a million times better than sex.'

'No!!?' I had no idea what to say, I was anxious to sound enthusiastic.

'Antique coins, masses of antique coins, napoleons dating from before Napoleon,' he went on in a sing-song voice, indifferent to his audience now, eyes in the middle distance.

'Real antique coins?' I put in, more to interrupt him and show I was still on my toes.

'Makes you think, huh? They're all with an expert now. Numismatist, know what I mean? I'm still doing taxi work because it's like when you win the lottery, you don't want to change your life. Look at Bernard Tapie, he changed his life, and it all came crashing down. Anyway, it'll be for my daughter. She's going to need it. You don't know what kind of world our kids will have to live in.'

'What've you put by for me, in fact?' came a sleepy voice beside me. 'Besides your ring, I mean? That won't get me far.'

'It will, you'll see,' I murmured. 'Don't be so envious the whole time.'

We were outside our place. I congratulated the driver on his treasure, he asked me again not to mention it to anyone. Of course not. We climbed the stairs with our packages.

I had to put everything down to fumble in my pockets for a key. Son and birds were inside in an instant, comfortably installed, Eugenio lying full-length in his overcoat, the cage under one arm, the television already on. Meanwhile I, the dummy with frozen ears, was still glued to the doormat, trying to pick up my parcels in the most rational manner possible. I never tired of practising tiny, personalized time-and-motion sequences, applied domestic ergonomics. Otherwise the brain went dead, I found.

The canaries seemed to like the flat immediately. They looked smug and, as it were, on the brink of song.

'I'm hungry,' Eugenio said. A pang went through me.

'Fancy a bird hunt?' I quipped.

'They're already prisoners, you slavering carnivore,' he replied with feeling. Quite touching, actually. 'Don't you think we should let them fly free in the flat?'

Without answering, I plunged into unwrapping and tidying away. That sort of thing needs to be done very quickly, I think, the minute you come in. Suitcases are the same, they need unpacking as soon as you step inside the door, otherwise there's no end to it. It should be done straight away and it should be done fast. Make room for what matters. It goes with making the bed when you get up, clearing the table as soon as the meal is over, not lolling about in a bathrobe and doing your hair and eye make-up before you go out. I have often wondered what secret conviction such rules spring from, what is being appeased. I call it making one's life into a work of art, that is the name I give my funny habits, the certificate I award myself when everything is in its place, forming a harmonious whole, a pretty room, a table decorated with a platter of fruit and a branch of lilac. I have to act, it seems to me, as if someone was about to ring the doorbell, or better still, come in without ringing. For that inspector — that private view, as it were — everything must always be tidy. Maybe he lifts the roofs off houses? The place that has to be set aside for him — in the mind, I mean — is like the bowl of food set out for the tramp who might call. Equally, people should have their affairs in order the day they die, which might be any time. But enough of that. The bird-cage, its inhabitants and its accessories were all in place. It was on with the show.

'Mummy, I'm hungry!' the voice in the next room repeated, stuck in a groove. 'Look, it's nearly half past two and I'm hungry, OK?'

Again, sweat broke out on my forehead. As if they were going to take Eugenio away from me as an incompetent mother, as if he were about to tell on me somehow.

'What do you want to eat?' I shouted in a steady voice. That kind of conversation calls for shouting, paradoxically it is more intimate, also it gives the impression you have a large apart-ment. 'Fish fingers all right?'

I took him a tray in front of *Little House on the Prairie*.

I turned up the heating slightly and sat down behind him.

'I love it when you make an armchair for me, mummy,' he announced, leaning back against my stomach. It was an emotional episode, with an old fellow reciting the Declaration of the Rights of Man. The birds had chosen a perch each and were fine. I began to explain to Eugenio the plan of campaign for the next few hours and days. He was not listening, because of the actor still going on about the merits of the equality of all men. Justice, Concern for Others.

There was an element of deliberation in choosing a bad moment to speak to him. It is a familiar failing of women, so consequently of mothers. Just an element, I think, no more than that. I love watching television with my son, but I find it impossible to concentrate. I think of other things, I talk to him, he doesn't listen, I lose patience, I start shouting, he starts shouting, I storm off, slamming our only door, and that's it, the honeymoon is over.

'It's because you're afraid of the climate of solidarity the child is seeking to establish,' Martha had once told me. Martha, a dental radiologist, had been my friend since schooldays.

She was undoubtedly right, I accepted that, it was what I liked about her — the courage to be right, to know the answer. Her blinkered rightness.

I needed to tell Eugenio that I was having dinner with Martha, who had issued an urgent summons.

'Eugenio, I'm having dinner with Martha,' I said, having first suggested a stroll in the park around four o'clock, 'and afterwards we'll see.' The name 'Martha' filled the room, permeating the air, turning it bad.

'And me?' asked my abandoned child, 'what about me? I'm always on my own. Even on Christmas Eve you leave me alone. Why do you prefer her? She's nasty, she makes you cry, can't you see her some other time?'

His outburst sent a pang through my heart. It also made me smile. Martha would have made the same speech, in her own way. I could almost hear her:

'Why do you always take your son's side against me? He makes you cry, he makes your life a misery, he's shutting off your mind, he's a selfish little tyrant. One day he'll go off without a word of thanks, he won't even say goodbye. I might not be there to have dinner with you. It's not doing him any good, you know, all this love, all this sacrifice and love.'

'I'm going to lie down,' I said to Eugenio. 'Secret of a long life, a siesta. Wake me up when it's time to go to the park.'

I curled up, making a sort of circular hollow in the middle of the bed. The birds trilled on their swings. A man on the television was droning on. I thought I caught the sentence: 'If you really loved your children, there'd be no more wars.' It made me weep as I started to slip away. But then, really loving, what do we know about that, I thought. And the thought took me into sleep.

It was the silence woke me up. The special silence that snow makes.

'It's snowing!' I called to Eugenio, who muttered something about people who have trouble keeping anything to themselves.

Something crisp and fresh. A modern variant on the eternal theme of woman as chatterbox. Where do they learn these things, I wondered. He mocked my wild imaginings about the chilly sweetness of the exquisitely crafted flakes. I know, kids have the pants bored off them in nursery school with stuff like that.

Eugenio was busy with his work of art, a road he was tracing in the carpet, a sort of labyrinthine landscape, a map of some country, possibly. I called it his Songlines. He was using a pair of small dressmaking scissors to sculpt the pile inch by inch.

'One day it'll be finished, and we'll have to move!' I had told Martha.

'What I find most amazing is that you do, after all, manage to cope.'

But I knew it was not sincere, her amazement. She was awaiting my downfall. Friends are nearly always like that. That is why, more often than not, you have none left when you get old. In fact, having no friends left is one of the best indications that you are at last (or already) an ancient. Each has demonstrated his or her failure, and you are left alone. No one is interested in anybody else any more, apart from the sick, the dead, those who are eventually awarded gongs. Every-one stays at home, safely bedded on failures forecast and confirmed.

We are all on the starting-line, up until the moment when we realize that's it, the race we had so looked forward to has been held without our noticing, the unrelenting race of snails towards their wonderful giant lettuce leaf.

'Come on, we're going to the park!' I told Eugenio firmly.

'Oh, why?' he whined, drawing out the last word as long as

possible. 'What's the point? Let's stay here! It's snowing, you don't like snow, and I don't like going out.'

I knew we should go out. Get some fresh air. It was one of the few maternal certainties I had made my own. Get some fresh air every day. Whatever happens. Go to the park, stay there till you feel despair begin its irreversible dirty work. I assumed it was why other people went to church, or went shopping. Question that and you undermine everything. For years, I had taken the pushchair out every single day and zigzagged between the bared teeth of dogs and the belching exhaust pipes.

Nowadays, we held hands, and I told Eugenio the names of the statues we passed. I taught him to spot the ribbed vaults of carriage entrances and to study people. People walking, people waiting and, my favourite victims, those who think they are invisible in their cars.

The day before, for example, a young woman who had bought herself a very pretty lacy dress had been holding it up at the traffic lights. Cocking her head, she made it dance before her eyes. It isn't every day you see something so joyful. It gives the same sense of delight as a shell or a bit of smooth glass on the beach, or a new path in the woods.

'Voyeurism and depression,' Martha had said when, some months before, I had told her of my earliest exploits. So, from then on, I'd kept them to myself.

Eugenio put on his anorak, filling the pockets with various bits and bobs. I half throttled him with his scarf, the one that scratches and smells, and out we went.

The park was a vast brown pool of ice and snow.

'I've never seen it so sinister!' I told my son delightedly. 'We're two trappers in the Frozen North. Look, not a soul in sight! It's like when I was a girl: we used to go to the beach in all weathers, it strengthens the character.'

'Trappers with no dogs, no sledge and no whisky are twits,' Eugenio observed. 'Dead twits, even. And just because you were tortured as a child, don't feel you have to take it out on me. What have I done? Nothing. In fact, I never even asked to be born!'

That stopped me in my tracks.

It was something Eugenio loved saying, he thought it sounded really good, borderline metaphysical but simple with it. To me, it was an empty form of words, hollow and unpleasant. Afterwards, we sulked, lips pressed so tight they might have cracked. The snow crunched under our lamentably permeable soles, we were not only taking in fresh air at one end, we were absorbing water at the other. It would be so comforting, I thought, to go and buy Eugenio some leather boots. The feeling of security this induced brought a flush to my cheeks, and I smiled at my son. He had extracted a tiny disposable camera from one of his huge pockets.

'Do you think I can photograph snow as it falls?'

Everything was still and much too silent. The very cold was silence. The bare, brown, cold earth was silence, so was the frozen water. The green gates were the most human thing there.

A sparrow broke the oppressive stillness, skidding on a small puddle. Eugenio ran at it, machine-gunning. Suddenly, intensely, there was an atmosphere of adventure, gone in an instant.

'Come on, mummy, let's go home, please, can we go home now?'

I realized, from the nature of the request, that Eugenio was growing up. He had never been willing to leave the park before. And I, who hated the place, found myself missing the days when only pulling him by the hair would make him abandon his waterlogged sandpit, his rusty bucket, his little split shovel.

Going home, we took the metro.

Foreheads pressed to the glass of the rear carriage, we watched the tunnel lights slip away, we were astronauts at lift-off. The metro, I used to enjoy telling Martha when we had dinner together, is our territory, our poetry. Eugenio would collect all the articles I brought him about crickets lurking in the warmth, living off sandwich crumbs, about the latest indications of super-intelligence among urban rats, or about Saint-Martin station, which in winter is set aside for the homeless. He used to fold the tickets into endless accordions and dream of one day planting a red flag on a train that would burst out at Bir-Hakeim or Austerlitz and challenge God knows what, one of those old locomotives you see in westerns, probably.

I knew that, for all her sarcastic remarks, it knocked her out, our talent for wasting time, what she called our 'penny poetry'.

That evening I thought perhaps I would tell her about the

sparrow, if I remembered. You can never tell in advance what stories you are going to remember. This is a big problem, like dreams. And the ones you make a note of, so as to be sure, come out all shrivelled, like yesterday's oysters.

As we emerged from the station, a homeless person selling magazines latched onto us. I was cold myself, I didn't feel like mumbling a feeble 'Sorry, got one already.' I gave the man the ten-franc coin my fingers found in the bottom of a pocket, and he held out a copy.

'No, thanks. That's all right.'

I actually said those words. The man said something back, clearly displeased. We hurried away. Eugenio was livid.

'Don't you realize he's selling magazines to try to get back his dignity, and you humiliated him, you deliberately humiliated him. You made him into a beggar. I'd never have thought you capable of such a thing. You had no right!'

I was devastated.

'Eugenio, I'm devastated,' I said. 'I didn't want a magazine, that's all, I really didn't want one. His dignity would consist in not muddying the water like that. Or offering me things I don't want. Or begging without pretending not to.'

I was not as sure of myself as I sounded. I had just not wanted to give in.

We looked up together as we passed the Magnolia Palace hotel. Balconies were lit up, and against the blue night sky the blue, white and red flag flapped hugely. The snow had stopped, everything looked sharp and very splendid.

'It's beautiful, don't you think?' I murmured.

'I actually don't like flags,' Eugenio answered. 'Except the red one. Like dad. As for you, ever since you became a famous artist there's been no knowing what you like.'

I lacked the courage to deny it. Odd, though, hearing the words 'famous artist' sound like spittle in my child's mouth. I did not even flinch. I found it so hard to bear that there should be, inside Eugenio, a secret voice that bad-mouthed me and a corner of his heart that hated me in silence, so as not to hurt me.

We were home. Climbing the stairs, I hoped, as I did every day, as I did every time, trying not to look, that there would be something outside the door, lying on the mat, a spray of roses and eucalyptus, a bunch of periwinkle, a basket of fruit, a telegram from Michelangelo Antonioni. Or a little matchbox painted white to represent a mini-coffin, with a black cross painted on the top, sent by an ex-lover who has since gone mad. Actually, that last present I was not too keen on, I'd had one already.

As usual, there was nothing, not even a letter from the bank, not even a prize draw.

'Run along and feed your birds, entertain them, make them tame,' I said curtly, 'while I run your proletarian bath.'

We slid into the last waltz of our evening rituals.

3

The wind brought tears to my eyes, the night was turquoise blue. I was running. I was so sure I was late. Also, I was rehearsing my sparrow story for Martha, wondering whether to substitute a seagull or a pigeon instead. The hero of this version was Eugenio, image-hunter and poet. Stories are better and truer when you change them slightly. I was reminded of that film sequence where a man sees a little girl run out onto a frozen pond. He senses that the ice is going to split open and swallow her up. He is standing at his window, all he can do is watch. And suddenly I saw, through the windowpane, a sparrow hop out onto ice that was too thin. No sound would come from my throat, my hands were trembling. He had Eugenio's face. Suddenly terrified, my heart racing, I banged into one of those black bollards set at the edge of the pavement — to stop cars parking there, I think, curious things, mooring posts where no boat will ever tie up, serving no other purpose than to inflict surprise wounds on careless passers-by. Badly bruised, I began to cry. If the only way to understand the sea is to be shipwrecked, you've every hope, I told myself.

We had arranged to meet in a little stone basement with windows softened by stained glass, right opposite a Romanesque church standing in its churchyard. I liked that church because it used to display a crib with a real ox and a proper donkey flanking the mother and child. A real mother and a pretend child.

I used to like going there over and over again, maybe a dozen times, and each time I would wonder how they managed to stand so still.

I liked Christmas cribs, quite as much as animated window displays in big stores, yet I never showed Eugenio one. I liked the trembling and mystery in which the story of the donkey and the ox was embedded. I used to enjoy not wanting to know any more about it than the one word, crib, the smell of hay and the organ music in the background.

Then they stopped having a live crib. Instead, at Saint-Julien-le-Pauvre, they had a work of art designed collectively by Boulle School students. It was like salt dough, the baby had no face. I still popped in occasionally all the same, to light a candle that both illuminated the crib and gave me a wish. I remembered the girl who used to dress up as Mary, her head on one side, the blue veil hanging down and cramps in her knees, and she made me think of the art school I'd once attended where, under the industrious gaze of several old lady artists, a party of Japanese tourists left stranded by their coach and various ungrateful girls who were always breaking their charcoal because they pressed too hard, a wretched Polish woman, pink-cheeked, incessantly struck the same poses before a small electric fire, holding each for twenty minutes exactly, looking fed up. It was sad and it was miserable but at the same time it was extremely beautiful. I'd never taken Eugenio there either, though it would have amused him.

Perhaps if I did, I reflected, the desire to paint would come back.

Martha was late. I hesitated to sit down by myself. I retraced my steps with the idea of spending a moment in my church. The smell of incense caught at my throat, several people were gathered round the altar, singing. In the left-hand side aisle, a man in a parka was speaking in low tones to a Byzantine Virgin, lips almost touching her painted ear. He kissed her a good twenty times, planting the kiss on his fingertips and conveying it to the icon's gilded cheek. A tramp had installed his striped plastic bags in a recess, he mumbled insults at anyone who passed.

I lit a dwarf candle, spilling hot wax over my fingers for five francs. My wish. I could not think of one, only pathetic little wishes like hitting on something nice to do for Christmas. Or else too big: happiness, joy, no more of this, no more of that. Too late now, I realized — once you have put the candle down, that's your turn over.

Someone tapped me on the shoulder, I jumped.

'I knew I'd find you here,' Martha announced. 'Made your wish?'

'Didn't have time, they were all ...'

I could find no words, filled with self-loathing at lacking even the ambition to formulate a wish properly and in time. As we emerged from the little Greek basilica, I spotted furtive looks on the faces of two people leaving with us. A sort of complicity united us, a blend of pride and fear of being seen. I remembered how, on a visit to Rome, the same feeling of being involved in a plot had once accompanied me down the steps of Santa Maria del Trastevere. I had just attended a gathering of heretics, adepts of a ritual that must have pre-dated St. Paul. The chanting had been unforgettable, rather like the smell of incense inside Saint-Julien-le-Pauvre. Both made me think of love, which always hides and slips away.

Martha dragged me towards the restaurant, one arm clamped around my shoulders. Feeling fragile, I removed it.

In an exaggeratedly theatrical manner she declaimed: 'All right, you know what you should have wished for?'

'Stop it!'

I tried to make her laugh: 'Wishes are secret, Martha!'

I begged her, but she was inflexible. We were now sitting at a table, the lamp threw a cosy circle of light.

'A man, Nouk, you know perfectly well what you should be wishing for: a man. Yes, I'm talking about love, don't make that face, you look like a frightened doe. As if you didn't realize the truth yourself, you've banished love for love's sake, there's no room in your heart for anyone but your son.'

I tried to recover some dignity, the waitress was offering menus, I wiped my eyes. I wanted to go home.

'A touch harsh, don't you think?'

Martha did not reply but smiled at me fondly, she was very happy with us both. And with the new, slightly blond lock of hair in her fringe.

'A blond bombshell,' I told myself, to cheer myself up.

'That was just to put you on your toes! I've got so much to tell you.'

Her clear, penetrating voice became slightly muffled. I was thinking I would prefer, just then, not to know all her news. I lowered my head, glancing up at her sideways. As we waited for our food, I listened to what was being said at neighbouring tables. Meanwhile, Martha was describing a man she had met three weeks before: 'Three weeks, do you realize?'

Another man was sitting opposite, just ahead of our table. He had his back to us. Red nape, red ears, complaining noisily. I dubbed him, in my mind, the Red-Eared Fascist. For a moment I toyed with the idea that this was the prince whose secrets Martha was now so shamelessly sharing with me. But he was talking in a loud voice about a pregnant woman who had hit on this despicable ruse, he meant having a baby, to avoid being evicted from a flat he owned.

'They're pros,' he growled indignantly. 'You find them all over. Cockroaches.' I had to smile, such raw violence. For no reason.

'I know what you're thinking,' Martha went on.

What I like about Martha — she has many qualities, I mean what's specially nice about her — is that she doesn't, as I do, catch herself on the least little snag. In the beginning I would often phone her after our talks to apologize for annoying her and embarrassing her and undoubtedly offending her. She couldn't understand. My imaginings made her laugh.

'You have too much time on your hands,' she used to say good-humouredly, 'worrying yourself silly about things you've simply made up. Honestly, intellectuals! And your type of artistic intellectual is the worst, never not wounded in some way or other, never without something to upset them. What about painting joy for a change, ever thought of that?'

The reason why she said such things, I knew, was because she really did miss my painting career. What a farce that was! We live in a world where painting has become impossible. When I gave up the life, the private views, when I tore up my contract and broke with the gallery people, it took me months to own up to Martha. I was afraid she would leave me too, after Alfonso, after all the others. But Martha was loyal, she was stubborn. She watched over me. She was waiting for what she thought of as a silly masochistic whim to blow over. That would be her hour of triumph.

Every day, day after day, Martha sticks little squares of stiff cardboard in her visitors' mouths and tells them not to move, never for a moment suspecting the pain being inflicted by the corner of the cardboard digging into the patient's palate, quite unaware that it is all the patient can do not to throw up. Not bothering too much, either, about the fact that the march of technology will soon make her clumsy equipment obsolete. Her job is repairing weak jaws, and she does it with conviction. Hardens a person, must do. 'What a poet, and prissy with it!' she had sniggered after I had once tried to open her eyes to the sadistic side of her profession.

'I know what you're thinking, you're thinking it won't last, I'm dreaming as usual, Jason's taking me for a ride.'

'With a name like that, can you doubt it?' I sneered stupidly. Only to myself, though.

New names had an odd way of suddenly sprouting from Martha's lips, sounding almost as immodest as her confidences. It was a question of intonation. She said 'Jason' the way she would say: 'I'm going to show you where the treasure is buried that you've been searching for all your life.' I suddenly realized: if I am sitting opposite her, it's because I believe her.

I would have preferred her to ask me: 'What about you, then? What exhibitions have you seen lately?' The question you hear being lowered like a little gangplank between women having lunch together, showing each other their hands: 'Oh, but that show at the Grand Palais — fantastic, fantastic.' Such museum reports have always struck me as meant to inspire envy, or possibly mortification, in whichever of the two activists is doing less, starting to slow down, no longer following the listings. It is a way of staying on one's feet, asserting one's superiority. The next stage is when they begin telling each other about last night's television programmes. They may have lost a shred of self-respect by then. It is still culture, but sitting down.

The women at the next table had launched into this script. The larger, sheepish-looking one was taking stick for having seen nothing. Neither the Grand Palais, lined with Chardins, nor the Orangerie, with all those angels grinning dementedly, nor the new exhibition at the Louvre, works that may never be seen again but make good memories. I hate that game: collecting exhibitions, complete with comments drawn from the catalogue. It sets my teeth on edge, people putting on the style. Still, there's comfort in it, clearly. An obscene sort of comfort, like tourism. Which it is.

'Jealous snob,' Martha would have called me had I told her of these musings prompted by our loud neighbours. She was unaware of their voices, she saw no point in listening to conversations at other tables.

'It interests you because you're scared to live your own life,' she must have told me a hundred times. 'It's like your bloody books!'

Abruptly, Martha thrust her face close to mine. It was alarming, she might have been about to kiss me. I looked away. At the same time, something made me laugh: I imagined her saying quietly: 'Your breath stinks.' Yet I had checked a hundred times on the way there. Bad breath is an obsession with me. I'm always huffing into cupped palms, sniffing in the warm, sickly-sweet air that comes back at me. She said: 'Do you think I'll be happy? It's so powerful, what's happening to us, so violent. I've never known love-making like it is with him, and when he kneels in front of me, like he did last night, I think I'm going to die. Before, with Étienne, it seems to me it wasn't love, just a kind of mutual masturbation, each of us after our own pleasure. And each of us then achieving pleasure, coming at the same time, purely from friction, know what I mean?'

She wasn't looking at me properly any more, she was beaming into space. 'When I think we've been married nine years. You know, he has enormous respect for Jason?' My lips curled with pain.

'And Jason ...' I wished she'd at least stop saying his name. It scared me. The police could arrest us for serious indiscretion, violation of privacy, verbal exhibitionism in a public place. 'When he takes me and makes me come over and over and over ...'

'Please, Martha, stop it,' I told her. 'I'm very fond of you, and you will be happy, he loves you, I'm sure of it. But it's dangerous, what you're doing. There's nothing to be said about Jason and you that the whole world hasn't known since the beginning of time, and the secrets of the bedroom should stay secret, of that I'm sure. Anyway ...'

She was still staring: 'You know that way of coming and coming without ever wanting it to stop, and then finishing together? It's because you're my friend, Nouk, that we talk like this, we want to share our secrets, and also because my happiness is not complete if you don't know about it.' I was a worm wriggling in her fingers. I felt tipsy with fright and ridicule.

'Don't play the neurotic,' I heard her reproving me, 'it's just cowardice, laziness.'

I was not crying. Actually, I found it rather amusing, this forced march towards happiness. Only there was a problem of vocabulary. A big problem. We have hardly any words of our own left, they are all written on invisible autocues, hard words, too hard for our mouths but that have to be said anyway, even though they're as harsh as they are empty. They take the skin off. It's the same with painting. I felt I had to make Martha see that I would never lift a paintbrush again. She had to give up thinking I would get back to it some time. I knew I must stop her, once and for all, tackling me about it at every opportunity.

'I've sold my last pictures, Martha, for almost nothing. You know? Do you remember what they were fetching three years ago? What a joke! I don't feel up to all that affectation any more. I'm ashamed of my paintings, as if they were something I'd puked up. All that anguish, auctioned off, prostituted, it's so ... Anyway, has there ever been a woman painter who was worth the candle? I don't think there's anything for me any more in that direction. All my illusions have vanished. I'll never paint again.'

'I believe Étienne would like to see you,' Martha put in, pink-cheeked now. 'That's another thing I wanted to talk to you about. You've always been very close, you two. Idealists. Good people.'

Verdicts like that are always handed down with a sprinkling of scorn. Behind 'idealist' I understood 'stupid', behind 'good' there was more than a hint of 'feeble'. Martha, in the nicest possible way, grasped my hands. They were too cold.

'You'll call him?'

'Of course,' I said, 'I'll give him a ring tomorrow.'

Maybe she hadn't heard — about the painting, I mean. Or perhaps there was simply nothing to be said. 'Pull yourself together! Have a little faith in yourself!' Martha would have groaned ordinarily. 'The best compliments, the only ones worth paying, are the ones you owe yourself, that's what my grand-mother used to say. "Work, work, work. When you've gone, the world will get on fine without you."'

I wondered who would come to my funeral.

Tenderly, nostalgically, I thought of Eugenio, of our calm ship, its monotone landscape. Listening to Martha was making me sea-sick, giving me that strange feeling of being unable to lean against anything, being surrounded by walls that my arm went right through, trying to keep my balance on the sloping floor of a fairground attraction. I could hear onlookers laughing. Sheep, I told myself, chickens are braver than you. And I bit into a bitter black olive to seal the memory.

My attention was drawn to a couple two tables away, as if here was to be the source of one of those truths that are always piercing me and about which I know only that they're what I'm looking for. ('It's your favourite word — *why*,' Eugenio would say when he was trying to please me.) The man's voice was too loud, too deep.

'Our memory is so selective,' he boomed. 'Also, the French are hopeless at geography.'

'That's me,' offered his ladyfriend, who had taken out a tiny mirror and was scrutinizing her face. 'I don't even know where Patagonia is, for instance.'

It was doubtless a way of saying: 'How handsome you are, darling!' And it worked a treat. Patagonia turned out to be one of the man's favourite subjects: the lightness of the Andean air, the pampas and the cactus, the cool South American breeze, he quoted Paul Morand, recalled his childhood, chickenpox, weeks of boredom, how he'd learned an atlas by heart.

Martha changed the subject. She wanted Étienne to meet more people, but it was difficult.

'He's just quarrelled with one of his few remaining friends. If he's all alone, I'll not be easy in my mind,' she stated baldly.

'Maybe that's what keeps us going, trying to find a way of being easy in our minds. Fortunately, we never manage it,' I said as kindly as I could.

'I've told him to sign up for something, you know, evenings, he just sits in front of the box. You know?'

Martha said 'box' as one might say 'unseeing'. 'He makes up his little tray, his flask handy.' She was also in the habit of saying 'flask' for 'whisky'. It took me years to understand what she meant. I didn't dare ask. I imagined, not thinking about it too much, something soft, a kind of second stomach.

'He's a zombie, I keep telling him, but he won't listen. You know?'

Whenever Martha started saying 'You know?' too often, I knew that my attention was too obviously wandering. Now, afraid of annoying her, I pulled myself together and started listening. 'Sorry, wasn't concentrating.' Like Étienne, whom I resembled, I was anxious not to risk losing Martha, my only friend, with whom I already had so many black marks. An honest person would have told her that being called a zombie day after day after day was not everything a boyfriend could wish for. But Étienne was not my boyfriend. I was interested in him, that was all. And that may have been because Martha told such good stories. Especially about ailments.

Étienne had some unique ones. Fascinating.

'How are his feet?' I enquired. For months he had been unable to walk on account of a violent itching sensation that had taken up residence beneath his feet, turning his arches and even the entire soles of his feet into seething ants' nests the moment he stood up.

If he lay down, hey presto, the feeling vanished. I suggested any number of microbiological solutions. I get very excited about that sort of thing. I proposed tricks like insomniacs make up. For instance: you make your body believe you have absolutely no desire to sleep. You don't get undressed. You don't go to bed, you don't make a cup of orange-blossom tea. You stay up and watch telly and suddenly, astonishingly, there you are, fully dressed, lights blazing, sound asleep. Armed with this experience, of which I was quite proud, I suggested Étienne go out in special slippers, or even in those non-slip shoes with dear little rubber pimples that you can get nowadays. Or the psychological solution: find out what was causing the itch. He didn't want to go out walking, but why? What was he after? No stubborn mule ever had itchy hoofs, I pointed out.

Basically, what I thought was: he's doing it to please Martha. But I couldn't tell them that. So I brought them creams. I went to the alternative chemist that had recently opened where the old bookshop had been, near where we lived. I'd been fond of that bookshop, I had been in the habit of popping in. I still was. The new shop was like an aquarium, all white and green. Skin was on the ground floor, shaving near the cash desks, haircare and spirit in the basement, rows and rows of shelves full of little bottles, tiny pots of vegetable extract. And you could find masses of plant creams for wrinkles in cheeks, on elbows, shea nut and sage, lavender to soften, algae for cleansing. One time I'd bought so much they gave me a huge umbrella, also green and white, like those old beach balls. I came out looking like Mary Poppins.

For now, Mary Poppins was gone. I felt wretched, actually, a sort of female Étienne, but showing no symptoms, apart from a strong desire to go home. Apparently, so a colleague at the library who was very keen on prison reading told me, people released at the end of a long sentence are reluctant to go out. Hostages feel friendship for their captors. We are mere bundles of habits, most of them fatal.

Martha was mashing her dessert, stirring it vigorously. The purée and the charlotte made a ghastly mixture. She laughed when I pulled a face. 'It'll be worse in a moment,' she remarked. Some people love the idea of food being all ground up in the stomach, ruining our efforts at presentation.

'What are you doing for Christmas?'

The question I'd feared most landed with a bump on the table between us.

'Nothing. Well, just the two of us. And a tree.'

'Have you bought the tree?'

'No, we're going tomorrow. All I've bought is some birds, because Eugenio wanted a cat.'

Martha gave me a puzzled look. In her place, I'd have supposed I was talking about food for the cat, preparing a welcome. She simply found me incoherent. And disturbing.

'You really are depressed. It's not good for a child, you know.'

Tears rose behind my eyes. I bit my lips. My retort was too loud, I was aware of flushed cheeks:

'It's not good to be *my* child, I know that, but the harm's done!'

The Red-Eared Fascist and the Patagonian Traveller cast surreptitious looks. Martha grasped my shoulders, hugging me, shaking me:

'What about this cat, then?' she asked, laughing.

4

It was midnight. I had to get back. We left the restaurant in a calmer mood, happy with the deal we had made: I would celebrate Christmas in my sad fashion, the two of us holed up in our little burrow, but as soon as it was over I would join them in Brittany, her and Étienne. There would be a wonderful crowd, and children, lots of children. We'd light fires, play Monopoly, eat cake, go for walks. 'You haven't been down for fifteen years. It's ridiculous,' Martha said.

I think she decided to invite us while I was telling her the story of the cat. Nice to think my love of stories is of some use.

And the story of the cat is one of my favourites — and one I can't ever use at the library during the Psychological Story Hour we hold once a month: it's too awful.

Chivalrously, I dropped Martha off. The taxi waited until she had tapped in the numbers and disappeared inside her modern building, all glass and metal, a spaceship equipped with three successive codes: one for the street door, one for the glass hall door and, finally, one for the lift. Tropical plants make a languid, gleaming corridor in the lobby, they look like extra-terrestrial spies, one's almost surprised that they are not fitted with lights and knobs. A lovely place, but you'd better not come home drunk. (I can't see how anyone, without all their wits about them, could carry out the many operations indispensable to getting to bed.) There have been several suicides, according to Martha, who accepts this with graceful casualness, insisting that one mustn't confuse cause and effect. That sort of building tends to attract frail personalities as the vacant shell attracts the hermit crab. A second steel skin. Tear-proof. I wondered briefly whether, in the Middle Ages, frail personalities became crusaders in order to qualify for a fine iron carapace that weighed a ton and the little visor that went with it. Where is our armour nowadays, I wondered.

The taxi dropped me, in turn, outside my own building. I looked up nervously. No light. Eugenio was sure to be asleep. The birds could be heard, no time was too late for them. Actually, I could only hear one bird.

Climbing the stairs, I thought of the cat again. *What about this cat?* Martha had insisted that the story did not ring true. She thought I had dreamt it. The cat had been called Freddy Buache. I can't remember why. We just used the first name. We called it Fred, or Freddy, or Freddo. Eugenio had been given it by his father a few days before Christmas, the previous Christmas or the one before that, I got confused. A kitten, all black, with blue eyes and a squint.

That year I had erected a little fir tree, all by myself, a real one that a girlfriend had given me, very thin and a bit lopsided. Freddy was delighted and promptly set about climbing it. As everyone knows, cats believe they can perch on the branches of trees because birds do. The tree bent, sprang back, the cat went flying, he promptly tried again. He managed to get a foothold on the nearby curtain, then he tried to use the bed as a springboard or trampoline. The needles began to fall prematurely, forming a green mat on the Turkish carpet. I left the vandals to their own devices. When I returned, the tree was on the floor, there was earth all over the place, Freddy was leaping about, and Eugenio was doing a drawing to express his undying affection for me in difficult circumstances.

I screamed. It was stupid of me, but I couldn't help it. Freddy and Eugenio both looked crestfallen. It was a dreadful night. Kittens, like babies, often have an inverted sleep pattern, I learned later. Around four in the morning, fed up with having a bouncy kitten on my bed and being taken for its ball, I decided that Freddy was only a cat and shut him in the bathroom, where he mewed pitifully without respite till morning.

'I hate that animal,' I told Eugenio.

'Mummy, you're so horrid,' was his straightforward reply.

'I know,' I said, as usual in such circumstances.

And I wrapped the remains of the tree in a big sheet, which I dragged down the stairs. I might have been disposing of the body of one of my victims. There was a trail of pine needles down the stairs all the same, but I'd recommend the method. And unwrapping the great skeleton on the pavement was hugely effective. It was when I got back upstairs that day that the business with the cat really began. Freddy was limping.

'Call a doctor, mummy, call a doctor,' begged Eugenio in tears. A doctor the day after Christmas, my heart began thumping the way it always does when a challenge looms that I know is beyond me.

I gathered him in my arms and kissed away his tears.

'Don't worry, your daft little cat has a needle in its paw, from all its acrobatics in the tree. Either that or it's sprained an ankle.'

Eugenio gave a shout of laughter: 'Cats don't have ankles, silly! Why not high heels, while you're at it?'

I love that expression: *'while you're at it'*. What could be sillier?

While I was at it, I phoned the emergency vet. It's just like the emergency children's doctor, only for animals. They take the time to talk to you, reassure you. Sounds silly, but it's time well spent, if you ask me.

'Someone'll be here in half an hour,' I announced.

Freddy mewed, his ears turned down like a tiny wolf. Eugenio thrust hundreds of toys under his snout, but without success.

'Stop squashing his face with those rubber things,' I commanded. I abhor sick animals. Not very nice, but there you are. We watched *The Aristocats* while we waited. Since Freddy's arrival, we had watched nothing else. *The Aristocats* is Disney's most boring film, but Eugenio said what did that matter?

'But I'm telling you, he won't watch, he doesn't understand and he couldn't care less,' I said spitefully. 'Why don't we watch *One Hundred and One Dalmations*?' I asked hopefully. 'For a change? I love that bit when he says: "I could eat, I could eat an elephant!" '

'What you mean is: you want to kill Freddy,' Eugenio said, indignant. A hundred dogs for him is like a hundred tigers for you. Or a hundred CRS.'

How he had found out that I was scared of the security police is a mystery.

In the middle of a love scene between the Duchess and her Thomas, the doorbell rang.

'Ah, *The Aristocats*, my favourite film!' the vet exclaimed as he came in, exactly as the emergency paediatrician would have done, used to taming situations swiftly. And he made straight for the basket overflowing with blankets. Of course, Freddy wasn't there. He hated that dust trap as much as I did myself.

Eugenio, a finger to his lips, pointed over at the bed.

'There he is,' he murmured, sounding like a doting mother.

The vet operated a kind of lure for cats, and stupid Freddy pointed his feverish little nose in the air. A firm hand grasped him. Eugenio and I looked on helplessly. Freddy, enjoined to take a few steps, limped pitifully as far as me and rubbed his head against my foot. 'A sprain,' the vet said. 'It happens with kittens. Not often, but it does.' Eugenio was proud of me. He knew I had wanted to study medicine.

'See?' he whispered, nice all of a sudden, 'you could even have been a vet.'

'Oh, I don't think so,' I answered in the same tone, seeing apocalyptic visions of a cowshed, a distressed animal, and me with my arm thrust in up to the shoulder to turn a calf that was lying badly.

Meanwhile the vet had opened an enormous bag. Actually, it was more a sort of giant instrument case, like in the old days, with clips to hold things. Inside the bag were dozens of little bottles and syringes, mostly filled with red, white, or yellow liquid and bearing tiny labels. In the middle of telling Eugenio a funny story about a calf with two heads, the vet grabbed a bottle, grabbed a syringe, grabbed the cat, and the thing was done. That was what he said:

'Done!'

At that moment, Eugenio gave a little cry. Freddy had gone all limp, he was either unconscious or dead.

'What have you done, exactly?' I asked the vet in my most sophisticated voice. I was thinking: 'You've killed him, you idiot!' Actually, I didn't really think that. I didn't dare. I was sweating and I could feel my heart in my stomach, still beating. I wondered what to do next, unable to get my mind round the situation.

He picked up the kitten, which was like a fur collar come unstitched. He sounded its chest. Eugenio and I looked on without breathing. No one was breathing — certainly not the cat, it seemed.

'Well?' I asked deliberately, sounding patriarchal and solemn (same thing, to my mind).

The vet found speaking difficult. 'He's in a coma.'

That probably means he's not dead, ran my instant mental note.

Eugenio was looking at us, weeping silently. He blurted out: 'I don't understand what you've done to him.'

'A medical error,' the vet replied, sounding worried. 'I don't know why. It's my first. Perhaps because of that scene in *The Aristocats*, my favourite love scene. Do you know, that's possibly why I took up this profession. I've just gone into analysis,' he added, turning towards me. 'It changes a lot of things in one's life, don't you think?'

I thought: 'He's not sure it was a big step forward, certainly for any kittens unlucky enough to cross his path.'

Eugenio had stopped crying and was studying the vet keenly.

'So you've killed Freddy, then? And that's it, nothing's going to happen, you won't be punished, it's allowed, killing cats, walking into people's homes and killing kittens with syringes and walking out again afterwards, that's allowed, is it? Say something to him, mummy.'

The vet tried to put his hand on Eugenio, which was not very clever of him. He said that Freddy was certainly not dead. Not at all. Just asleep.

'Like Sleeping Beauty, son, that's all, don't you see?' he said with a chuckle. A stupid image. 'I put him to sleep so that the sprain could heal, but I used the wrong dose, chose the wrong bottle. That was the one we use for large adult dogs, St. Bernards, Dobermans, Alsatians.'

'Will he sleep for years and years?' Eugenio asked, pacified now, caught up in the beauty of the situation.

'About twenty hours,' the vet said firmly. I was amazed that he could say anything with such confidence after what had happened. 'But listen, he absolutely must be shut in his basket and someone must be there when he wakes up. He'll have hallucinations and might do anything.'

Like shoot himself, I thought aggressively but said nothing. Everything was complicated enough already.

The vet left, not charging for the visit, and we spent the rest of the day keeping an eye on poor Freddy as we watched *One Hundred and One Dalmations* five times running. The next few days were even more ghastly. Freddy did not have a sprain, he had typhus. He fought every inch of the way and lost. He died after four days, the vet came back to see him from time to time, we were companions in misfortune. Freddy's fur was soaking wet, yet he refused to drink. For two days he mewed, then he no longer mewed, and that was even worse. I remembered now, it had been the previous year, and ever since I had resisted every attempt to touch my heart with lost kittens, doomed kittens.

We were always meeting them, and they all needed rescuing.
Clearly, I lacked the strength.

I turned the key. Each time I did it, I was reminded of friends
from the old days who often went out in the evening, leaving
their children alone. They said: 'There's more to life than kids,
one can't let family life swamp one, we're people too!' They had
always done it, they told people, so there. 'Nothing can happen
to a baby,' they said. 'At night, babies sleep, and if they cry
they'll get tired and stop eventually.' Later, they said: 'They're
big enough!' But they'd made a pact, and the father always went
in first when they came home. He would push open the door of
the children's room and say: 'All right, Madeleine, you can come
in, no corpses — yet again!' I no longer had someone to go in
first and I was always frightened when I opened the bedroom
door. I reassured myself with the story of Madeleine's husband,
imagining he would protect me. Eugenio sat up in bed. In a
suspiciously sing-song voice, he said:
   'You know, I think you're right about the Queen of England,
she must be pretty happy. I watched a television programme
about her castle. She has lots of birds.'
   And he went back to sleep.

You feel lonely when everyone else is asleep. I collected a pile of
magazines to look through for cuttings about our beloved queen
and put off thinking about the next day. 'Tomorrow's the 24th
of December,' I told myself, 'nothing special there, think Le
Mans (the 24-hour race), think about that film, *Twenty-four*

Hours in a Woman's Life, not even 24 times 24 sheep would get me off to sleep.' Every hour, a clock chimed. I studied all the Christmas Eve clothes, the latest ruses for keeping a flat stomach for a few hours, clay and capsules that wring out your guts. What faith a person must have in life to swallow all those awful and probably very dangerous things!

A little insert caught my eye. There was a photo of Elizabeth II, brocade dress, mouse-grey hat, small white curly-haired dog in her arms.

'The Queen of England has been the victim of an accident at her Balmoral home. The sovereign was slightly injured in the shoulder region by a pheasant falling from the sky. Experts point out that the accident could have been more serious, since a pheasant in free fall attains speeds of up to 40 kph.'

Balmoral Castle, with the queen sitting on the ground. Pheasant feathers on her dress. Horses tapping their hind hoofs. Smell of hunting. Falcons, possibly. The sea not far off, breaking on the rocks. I ran a bath, putting in seaweed. It made the water green.

Adam and Eve's cage stood on the windowsill. I watched them from the tub. There was something odd about them, something scary.

One of the two canaries was very much larger than the other. The lady in the shop had told us that was the male, large and aggressive, with tousled plumage, silky but tousled, and a strident song. He stared fixedly at the other canary, Eve, a little bundle of yellow and white, the female, bristling with terror and quite silent. He was blocking her access to the feeding-trough. But suddenly a doubt seized me. Maybe it was not the large one that was the male and the small one the female. Those were only projections, ways of conceiving strength and weakness. Maybe what I was looking at was a large cruel female, whom we had christened Adam, and a small put-upon male named Eve.

Adam did not actually attack the other bird, and the cage looked quite tidy. Eve sat submissively on the little top perch. Mute, trembling. Adam stared at her, waiting. I wanted to wake Eugenio, I feared the worst. A crime was unfolding before my eyes, I told myself, giggling stupidly. The seaweed bath suddenly disgusted me. Should I open the cage, or pretend I had seen nothing? I was inventing the whole absurd drama, surely? It was because it was late, this was Christmas, I'd drunk wine. Or because I'd been thinking about poor Freddy again, trying to be funny at the expense of Freddy's brief existence.

Shivering, soaking wet, I went padding in search of birdseed and attempted to sprinkle the weaker canary with a little hail of food. The larger bird sprang off its perch, and I stepped back. The seeds missed their target. The captor refused to let the victim budge.

'So,' I told myself, 'you're even capable of failing to help a canary of whom you had such high hopes.'

5

I woke to that Sunday-morning, holiday-morning silence outside. The sweet, dense Paris air was opaque with silence. Tree,
celebration, presents, the Christmas Eve meal: I felt a hint of
excitement, sufficient to push back the covers and toy with a
brief meditation about melancholy as a flood tide, and courage
as the dyke thrown up against it. I remembered the story of the
little Dutch boy who, out for a walk one morning, chanced to
discover a hole in the dyke protecting his village against the
grey waters of the North Sea, a tiny hole that threatened to
flood the polder. The boy put his finger in the hole, preventing
the water from escaping and so saving the whole countryside
from inundation. Just one little finger, belonging to one little
boy, sitting still in the cold, all alone, not knowing whether
anyone would come.

I wondered if he had not caught his death of cold, saving his
country like that. 'Oh, I can't remember,' I muttered, heating up
some water. Suddenly, the chill air of the kitchen was pierced by
a scream:

'Mummy! Eve's dead, Eve's dead!'

Eugenio's eyes were wide with fright.

'Why, mummy, why? What happened? Was she ill, do you think? Did she commit suicide, or did Adam kill her?'

On the shelf above the bath, all was calm — except, on the floor of the cage lay the body of the smaller bird.

'I don't know, Eugenio.' I could think of nothing to say to him.

Just then, the doorbell rang. On the landing stood a young man, slightly simple-looking, with dishevelled hair and cheeks blue with a two-day growth of beard.

Proudly holding out a bunch of white gardenias, tiger-lilies and tea-roses, he said: 'For you! Happy Christmas!' Eugenio was clinging to my hip. The florist saw that we were crying and, astonishingly, in an abrupt switch from triumph to concern, he asked: 'What's happened?'

'Nothing serious, don't worry.' I felt ridiculous. I could not even think where my purse was. I knew I should tip him.

I had felt Eugenio flinch as I uttered the sacrilegious words 'nothing serious'. Suddenly, he started talking to this complete stranger, talking as if to a friend, all because of the way the young man had asked his question, or for some other reason that I was unaware of.

'We had a bird die in the night. She was my Christmas present, we'd bought her together, my mummy and me, because afterwards the shops close, but I have no luck with animals, there was Freddy, who died last year, this time it was a pair of canaries, and they were going to be happy, have children, win singing competitions, they'd always be together.'

'Let me see your birds,' the young man said gently. He took

Eugenio by the hand and they went into the bathroom. The sun was shining on the cage now, and the surviving canary, feathers preened, was singing full-throatedly in an incredibly melodious voice.

'He's Adam,' Eugenio said. 'That one on the floor's Eve.'

Without a word, the florist opened the little door of the cage and took out Eve's body. He examined it carefully in the palm of his hand, then wrapped it in a paper handkerchief, slipped it into the breast pocket of his overalls and led us both into the kitchen.

Taking Eugenio on his knee, he began to talk to him. The water was boiling, so I made tea. Adam could still be heard in the background, and the canaries in the stairwell were now swapping trills and warbles and cooing defiance.

'Eve was not a female canary,' the florist said. 'He was a male. A small one, but a male all the same. The man who sold them to you made a mistake. It happens increasingly. They're not taught even the rudiments of the job any more. He's the one who murdered poor Eve without even touching him. Eve's presence in the cage was a provocation for Adam. Adam wouldn't let him eat or drink, that's how he killed him. It's nature.' His voice had risen as he spoke, becoming quite impassioned. I hesitated to point out that the man who sold us the birds had in fact been a woman, I was afraid of complicating matters further.

'I hate them, they're incompetent, irresponsible,' the young man muttered angrily. 'It's typical, everything's like that nowadays, crimes for no reason.'

I looked at him in amazement. It did not sound like a sermon or a ready-made rant, his anger, and there was I thinking indignation was an old people's thing, no one got indignant any more, certainly not florists. Which just goes to show, yet again, that we always get it wrong — yes, it's you I'm talking to, all you Sovietologists, seismologists, leader-writers, the hacks who write comment columns about the decline of youth, the people who tread the corridors of the Academy of Manners and Customs.

'We have to punish Adam,' Eugenio said. 'Could you help me kill him? I wouldn't know how to do it. Strangling's out, birds don't have necks.'

'First we must bury Eve,' the florist commented, without reacting specifically to Eugenio's suggestion. 'I ought to get back, actually, they'll be wondering what's happened to me. There's a bit of ground behind the shop, we use it to dump branches and trees and boxes. We could dig a grave for Eve there, if you like. He'll be all right there, surrounded by all the flowers that have started to wilt. In fact, he'll be fine. With your permission, ma'am, I'll take your son, we'll perform the ceremony, and I'll bring him back to you.'

I felt the taste of earth in my mouth: a dead bird, an anonymous bunch of flowers that smelled too strong, a stranger suggesting a burial ceremony. 'Be an adult,' hissed one inner voice. 'Do something. Say: "No thank you, you've been marvellous." Come, Eugenio.' And the other muttered: 'How does he know such things, this delivery boy? Ask him!'

'Mummy, we have to go, you have to come,' Eugenio said, very lively all of a sudden.

'I would just point out that we're still in our pyjamas,' I replied, blushing because I had only just noticed this myself, and if there is one thing I hate it's being caught in a state of undress. It scares me, as if street clothes and make-up were a shield against violence. Against judgements, too.

'We'll get dressed and we'll be along directly, sir,' Eugenio said.

'Right,' said the delivery boy. 'My name's Anton, my mother was a great fan of Anton Chekov, a Russian writer who wrote a lot of plays. Sorry, you probably knew that. Yes, well, the address is on the flowers. It's just around the corner.'

He left, having first placed his teacup in the sink and thrown a reproachful glance in the direction of the flowers, which I had not yet put in a vase.

We arranged our flowers. Eugenio enjoyed helping me. That was something my mother taught me, doing flowers. You pick up the flowers one by one, patiently, and pop them in. They will automatically assume the proper angle, with a tiny mystery surrounding each stem, it's just like harmony. Afterwards, if the arrangement works, it will fill the whole room with its secret beauty, its tranquillity and of course its perfume.

'Who can have sent us flowers?' I asked Eugenio. We were putting on our coats to go round to the florist's, the flat was almost tidy, and Adam was singing in the bathroom, sounding more glorious than ever.

'I'd like it to be dad,' he said in a very quiet voice, looking bravely up at me. And my heart burst. But he went on, sounding a trifle pretentious: 'You, I know, would like it to be some splendid secret lover, perhaps Federico Fellini himself.'

'He's dead, actually,' I replied with dignity.

'Brad Pitt, then?' Eugenio suggested mischievously.

'Quite possible. We'll know soon enough,' I concluded, slamming the door. Not dwelling too much on the fact that I rather thought I might be mixing Brad Pitt up with someone else. We were going to a funeral, after all.

'What are we going to do afterwards?' Eugenio asked. 'It's Christmas Eve, remember, we haven't got a tree yet, there are no decorations in the flat. Plus I don't want to be bored all day. I want you to think up something unforgettable, you can when you try.'

Surely I hadn't taught my only son self-interested flattery? Who had, then? And if it was me, how?

I pointed out that we were on our way to a florist's, which was a good place to start looking for a tree.

'After that, we'll see. I'll take you shopping at Bon Marché, they have a super food hall, bound to be masses of really wild things to eat for Christmas, African food, *and* it's open on Sunday.'

Eugenio grumbled that I was not getting off that lightly. A burial followed by shopping for groceries hardly qualified as an unforgettable Christmas Eve.

The flower shop was almost invisible from the street, no sign, and windows dotted with flakes of cotton wool, like in the old days. Inside, there was a sort of jungle, a narrow path between rubber trees and banana plants, a block of Christmas trees standing at the back, and huge clay pots, jars two metres across, filled with every variety of azalea, petunia, rose, tulip and freesia, which to me is the most touching flower of all. Behind a stockade of canes and bamboos, Anton and his acolytes could be seen lining up trees on the floor, a curious sight. Eugenio, jumping for joy, went over and crouched down with the others. I just stood there, very ill at ease, red nose, red hands, eyes watering.

'I've got our tree, mummy, I've got it!' Eugenio shouted after a few minutes. It was a great fat thing with masses of branches. 'They agree, they're giving us a discount!' The eleventh-hour Christmas tree, I thought.

They nailed two cross-pieces on the bottom to make it stand up, then stuck it in a corner while we held the ceremony.

There was a little grassy plot, it reminded me of my first garden.

I was nine years old, and it had seemed educational to teach me about patience and nature (the same thing, really) by planting tulip bulbs, crocuses and radishes. That had been what I wanted. I had ticked off pictures in a seed catalogue that had a posh name and was all irises, pansies and gladioli — stupid, pretentious flowers like that. I hoped to God they would never grow in my garden. My flower-bed resembled a grave. There was only the cold, damp surface of the earth, which I raked with gloomy thoroughness to get rid of all the twigs, stones and mole turds. I kept it up for two years, at the end of which time a few crocus tips did make a cautious appearance. Every grave since has reminded me of that flower-bed.

In the middle of the little grassy plot, inside the obligatory shoe-box, prone on a bed of cotton wool with violets at each corner, lay Eve. I was touched by these childish attentions. We sang a couple of Eugenio's favourite songs.

Afterwards I had a good excuse to go. We said our thank-yous and left with the tree.

'Why do you always rush off as soon as we make some friends?' Eugenio asked.

I said nothing. I didn't know why, it wasn't true, anyway we could hardly discuss it carrying a huge Christmas tree uphill.

We formed the usual procession. I carried the foot, the heaviest end, at least I thought so, and Eugenio the crown, with enormous joy. He sang. As we went, I began telling him (for perhaps the hundredth time) the story about the two cat friends and the hole they made in the ceiling for the tree to poke through, giving the mice in the attic a treat.

'Mummy, you'll never grow up if you go on telling the same children's stories over and over again. You'll just fade away, all wrinkled and old and tiny. Better watch out!' my son told me, puffing slightly, the top branches scraping along the pavement.

'Watch out for what?' I hit back, outraged. 'We are never betrayed but by our own, said Anaxagoras of Thrace. As for me, I find the hole-in-the-ceiling story most instructive, Your Honour. Let us examine, if you will, this business of the Christmas tree, this unforgettable image of the little round hole sawn in the ceiling to avoid having to crop the tree, a house built round a tree rather than the other way about, the treetop making a tree for the mice in the attic. Can you not see the subversive aspect?'

'You really are getting past it. It's time you changed your job. The library's not doing you any good, all those ...' Eugenio sighed, picking up his burden without finishing the sentence. I appreciated his occasional tact.

'My hands are all sticky with resin, are yours?' I said, feeling warm towards him.

We were nearly there. It was a time of freedom and joy — and of complicity: I enjoyed the way people watched our little procession pass.

An old woman with turned ankles, one bandaged knee, her body wrapped in threadbare cloaks like an old cat's fur, called out to us. We had put the tree down, it was like a Charlie Chaplin film. She was thrusting envelopes into the letter box at the corner of the street.

'I'm posting letters,' she laughed, 'but they're not addressed!'

'She's mad and she smells dreadful. You can't even tell what it is, the smell,' Eugenio muttered. 'Scary!'

'Did you hear what she was saying? Like a sort of riddle,' I pointed out to him. 'This could be the Sphinx itself, how do you know?'

Beside the woman was a barrow, the kind street traders use, looking as if it was collapsing under the weight of plastic bags, an unsteady pile of objects wrapped in bits of cloth and newspaper, a frying-pan with a hole in it, a string of tiny saucepans, toys, dozens of pullovers of matted wool, tubes of cream, cough-sweet packets, unidentified bundles, bunches of felt pens. A teddy bear peeped from a carrier bag. Tins of preserves, tangles of string, a cracked tray and the legs of a stool crowned this rickety pile.

The woman went on: 'They've all gone away, but the taxman don't know that. These are their tax returns. Always at Christmas they get their reminders, and it's me doing the posting, it's me, yes it's me! Good job I'm here!'

Eugenio's right, I told myself, she is simply mad. There's no metaphor here, no magic, just a batty old woman, someone on the scrap heap. What an awful thing to say! So useful, though, for pulling the door to behind you, forgetting. Yet if the whole scene made no sense, how come he was so frightened, and I felt so close to such rootlessness, the woman's obsession with little packages, the wrapped life, the whole parody?

'Come on, get a move on,' I said to my son, 'any more of this mooching about and it'll be another day for the dustbin.'

I enjoyed saying that, I must admit. It made me laugh a lot.

To decorate the tree, we took the stepladder, it's the only way, and hung up everything we could lay hands on. We had the usual box full of glass balls, many of them cracked but still kept on from previous Christmases. The tinsel garlands were beginning to go bald, and there were quantities of ornaments of varying degrees of originality.

Eugenio knew them by heart and had a special affection for some nasty little baked-clay figures decorated with beads that we had made over the years. There was even a string of red and green lights that blinked on and off. The late Freddy Buache had allowed a small number of our finest balls to survive. Made of some unknown substance, they were painted bright red and hung from gold threads — heavenly.

When the tree was entirely covered with decorations, we stood back to study the effect.

'It's the prettiest I've ever seen!' Eugenio said, pressed against my side.

'It's perfect! We've never done it so well.' I returned his hug, in fact I went one better. There was even a star on top, like a little hat on a lady. A good Christmas tree ought to look like a child's drawing. In drawings, there is always a star.

With the tree finished, we felt boredom and embarrassment about to descend on us.

'I think you've forgotten to get us a meal again, mummy,' Eugenio teased.

'I wish I could!' I laughed and gave him some ham and leftover pasta shells popped in boiling water for two minutes. Not bad for a Christmas Eve lunch. Sitting under the tree, we wiped our paper plates with white bread that was one hundred per cent chemical. And we savoured, I think, without knowing it, the beauty of the world.

'What's your idea, then?' asked the sucker of my lifeblood.

The paper plates were cleared away, the flat looked lovely, I felt idle and at ease. In front of us the red curtain, which I had raised up on either side, lent a touch of solemnity to our words. Outside, the small green scene steamed vaguely in the fine and probably ice-cold rain. The path in the carpet wound towards the tree, which shone with all its electric lights. I thought fondly for a moment of the Aborigines and of the old days when I had quietly studied their secrets before resigning myself to the card-indexes, regular hours, salary scales and phantoms of the library. That so recent epoch when I had not been aware that time is a cruel trap for dreamers.

Adam the Hardhearted was probably asleep, the ceaseless singing from the cage in the stairwell could be heard in the distance.

'Right. Three things,' I told my little Christmas soldier. 'The surprise and two chores, in any order you like.'

The time you waste discussing trifles! I heard the childrearing spies mutter behind me. They never leave me alone and they never shut up.

'Chore, surprise, chore!'

There's education for you, that swiftness of decision!

So we began by organizing Adam's temporary exile. It was what Anton, the florist-undertaker, had recommended: a kind of trial by ordeal, which had Eugenio slightly worried.

'Why not put him in with the other birds that sing in the

stairwell?' Anton had suggested. 'If your Adam is a real killer, they'll get rid of him. If not, he'll be happy. But don't keep him where he is,' he'd advised me, 'the lad will think about him constantly!' And I had imagined Eugenio getting up at night and slipping in where the cage was, penknife in hand, to avenge poor Eve. Anton had added with a slightly smug smile: 'Out of sight, out of mind.'

'But there'll still be his singing,' I objected.

'No problem. The proverb doesn't say: "Out of earshot",' Anton retorted. This really was a quite exceptional person, I decided.

So we laboriously removed Adam, his seeds and his rock out to the cage in the stairwell. I had the heady sensation of being a circus girl doing her lion-taming number. Adam obeyed my commands instantly and slipped into the king-size cage, pure white amid the six other canaries, who were all yellow or striped. Adam promptly occupied a swinging perch near the top of the cage and launched into one of his singing exercises, which was taken up in chorus by his hosts.

'They don't seem to realize they've got a killer amongst them,' Eugenio remarked, a bit disappointed. The taste for blood is soon acquired.

'Quick, put on your swimming-trunks, I'm taking you to Aquaboulevard!' I said then. We stuffed things into a large bag and jumped into a taxi.

Aquaboulevard was one of our dreams, we had never been there. Eugenio talked about it all the time, and I'd been a fan since seeing the advert in the cinema: a real beach, real waves, slides at least a kilometre long, all in the midst of a kind of jungle, with jacuzzis beneath palm trees. You saw a colourless secretary type, caught in a sort of blizzard one winter evening in

Place de la Concorde and completely drenched, change into a playful nymph simply by passing through the automatic gate of Porte de Vanves underground station, simply by entering this magical complex — called, mysteriously, Forest Hill.

We took a taxi. I admit it, to my shame.

'You'll get your son into bad habits,' a colleague at the Education Library had informed me the day I had unwisely talked about an outing of this kind. 'He'll think taking a taxi is the natural thing to do. Don't forget, we have some of the finest public transport in the world. It's there to be used, you know.'

I said that in southern countries there are taxis everywhere. I told her taxis were my greatest luxury. I mentioned that no one criticizes people who take the car out without an excuse, their little private car that they have all to themselves, with the smelly tartan blanket and the stuff lying on the back seat that's been there for ever, and those people cheerfully kill three hundred victims a year through air pollution alone. I heard it on the news. No one says anything to them about the bad example they are setting with their irresponsibility.

The taxi that took us off to paradise that day was driven by a sort of puce Smurf in a rainbow-coloured woolly hat with clumps of black hair sprouting from beneath it. He turned towards us a round face embellished with whiskers in the oddest places. On anyone else you would have called them eyebrows or a moustache: on him they were a kind of untidiness. He stared at us through enormous bifocals that gave him eyes like a fly and, while narrowly missing a venturesome pedestrian, an ill-sited lamppost and a piece of pavement that stuck out awkwardly, he began to speak, waving his arms about and wrinkling his brow in a way that made him look livid.

'You know the best way to pick up a woman?'

Positively braying with merriment, our driver went on to explain. 'Because it's Christmas Eve, right, and it's a Sunday, don't ever forget it! OK, the way to pick up a woman, there's nothing to it, just tell her the exact opposite of what she is. If she's ugly, say: "You're the most beautiful woman in the world!" If she's stupid: "You're a genius!" They believe it every time! The more it's untrue, the more they believe it!'

'Why is he telling us all this?' Eugenio asked me in a whisper.

'I don't know. I don't think it's particularly for you and me,' I answered, also whispering, and rather bewildered. Maybe my friend had been right, I thought, and one oughtn't to take taxis with a child who's old enough to follow the conversation.

'And another thing, do you like Depardieu?' the driver went on, abruptly turning glum. 'You're the sort who would.'

We were getting close to the undistinguished concrete complex that houses Aquaboulevard. Muttering an inaudible, hypocritical *yes-no*, I took out a fifty-franc note, ready to leap from the trap.

'Because I don't. I can't stand the man,' I heard the driver continue as we ran off, 'I hate him and I have good cause. It was through him my wife left me!'

'Is that true, do you suppose?' Eugenio asked, stuffing his hands into his pockets. We were forcing our way through the bitter wind that always seems to go with concrete paving.

He had beaten me to it. In a case like that, the first to ask wins. I said: 'Do you?' with what I tried to make a ruminative air but which came out as a mere grimace of cold.

'Yes, I think it's true!' Eugenio said firmly, and imagining the drama of Depardieu, the taxi-driver and the taxi-driver's wife quite cheered us up.

Accessing our dream meant walking through a kind of modern station concourse, past about a hundred metres of sports shops, their windows full of synthetic red-and-white swimsuits, all with plunging necklines. There were also balls of many kinds, boxing-gloves, sweaters and rackets, tennis shoes and trainers, coloured tracksuits and arctic jackets, purple weights, huge medicine balls to build up the muscles of the inner thigh and develop the pectorals, a whole expanding universe dedicated to the new. You can tell, somehow, when a business has the wind in its sails like that. 'It's like a toyshop for grown-ups,' Eugenio told me. 'I bet it has that same smell inside.'

At the end of the concourse we entered a long passage that smelled of asbestos. We descended two escalators, took a couple of turnings and crossed another hall full of those photobooths that immortalize you with one of the Hundred and One Dalmations in your lap and Snow White beside you. Further on, a row of fizzy-drink dispensers was followed by a self-service sweet display, where we simply had to buy two hundred grams of pick-and-mix, great big sweets, brightly coloured, beautifully sticky and soon forming a single clump.

'Sweets nowadays are like nothing on earth!' I told Eugenio with undisguised scorn and a fond thought for the humbugs and aniseed balls we used to buy.

'This is Radio Nostalgia, Frenchmen speaking to Frenchmen,' he chanted, quickening his step.

'Hey, when did you start quoting General de Gaulle?' I asked, all excited.

'Who's General Degole? I'm talking about the jingle in a funny cartoon you wouldn't have seen: the adventures of a bat called Golda. She's a radio ham. You'd like it, actually: Golda's a very brave girl-bat, and she's a colonel. Colonel of helicopter battalions. She's always saying: "Frenchmen speaking to Frenchmen".'

I said nothing. We were there.

'Look, you can see the waves!' Eugenio shouted. Below us, through a vast plate-glass window, a sea of heads surged up and down in time to a huge swell (I'm sure the designer got the idea from a Hokusai print) that eventually slammed against the end of the pool. It made you think of the Ganges, because of the splashing, slapping crowd, but a cartoon Ganges somehow.

'All it needs is a few bats!' I said to my son, who threw me a suspicious look.

The system of cloakrooms and lockers, which I have no doubt was the pride of the pool's creators, took quite some understanding. A maze of six-figure combinations, doors that opened only when others were closed and your coin had been inserted. A sort of hygiene front.

It all seemed justified up until the moment when you plunged into the vast, collective, over-heated bath that is Aquaboulevard. Suddenly, everything became clear: hygiene was outside, danger within.

These 'tropics' were like the metro, the crowd on the metro, the smell of the metro, the same promiscuity, the same materials, even. I'm in the metro, I thought despairingly. Naked in the metro. The worst of it was that the other passengers, usually so well wrapped-up, were also naked, really almost naked, because thongs were in fashion. Boils appeared to be in fashion, too. And people must have had about four legs apiece, there were legs everywhere.

'I'll see you, mummy, all right?' Eugenio shouted. He was already running across the tropical concrete surround towards the vast tropical wave and its clamouring crowd. I jumped into the water, jumped into that virtually pure bleach, that stinking chlorine, trying to pinch my nostrils, trying to banish the unpleasant image of too many bodies too close together. Water, I realized, is a less efficient separator than air. The feeling was one of sharing a bathroom with five thousand strangers.

The light in this paradise even had that yellowish, sinister quality cast by the bulbs you often find in bathrooms. Thanks to this arrangement, everybody looked ugly, pallid and badly built.

Once, at eighteen, I climbed the Acropolis along with fifty thousand other rubbernecks, and I shall never forget the feeling of death and disgust that seized me when I saw those coaches spewing out their loads of shorts and thighs, baseball boots with ankle socks, cameras bobbing on bulging stomachs, and braying ecstasies, noses in guidebooks. Next year we're doing Etna! I know there are too many of us on this earth, but sometimes it really hits you. You have to make an effort not to imagine all those grinning faces lined up dead, a cemetery waiting to happen.

'You've got your ant look again, mummy!' Eugenio shouted helpfully. He was now bounding around me like a sea-lion that has spotted a fish. Each kick delivered half a litre of chlorine into each eye. 'You wouldn't be cooking up some theory why you should never bring me here again, I hope. Because I'm warning you, I love the place! I've already made a friend, and we haven't been on the giant slides yet. Come on, stop brooding, you'll enjoy it!'

There was a pause. I rubbed my eyes, not thinking of anything, of eye lotion, possibly. My son looked me up and down.

'You didn't choose a very nice costume, the neck's too low, and that green's awful. Where did you find it? Plus it's all shiny. Luckily that doesn't show in the water, you must wrap a towel round yourself when you get out, you might want to go to the bar for a smoke.'

'Too kind,' I muttered. And I followed them, him and his new friend, over to the famous slide that had to be experienced before one died.

It was good. Not too fast, not too slow, really good fun. The only thing wrong with it was the twenty-minute queue and the shouts of the supervisor responsible for controlling the flow. 'No going down in groups, no one under twelve using the slide unaccompanied, here, how old are you?' We might have been in a police station.

'What's your friend called?' I asked Eugenio between slides. He gave me a withering look.

'I don't know.'

'Oh, I see.'

'What does it matter?'

'It doesn't.'

I left them to their love affair and returned to the 'beach' area.

Choosing a deckchair that stood a little apart, I took out a cigarette. Cigarettes smoked after coming out of the water have always been my favourites. I got out my bedside book, *Men in*

Dark Times by Hannah Arendt, and opened it at a poem of Bertolt Brecht's, 'The Ballad of the Secrets of Everyman'. The first two lines read:

We all know what a man is. He has a name.
He walks down the street. He visits the café.

And they plunged me into a profound daydream, as if those four sentences spoke volumes about my spectral presence that Christmas Eve Sunday, sitting all alone, almost lost, in fact, indistinct in my green swimsuit, slightly irresolute in my green skin, on the concrete surround of a giant swimming pool. I began to mumble a little song:

Nobody knows what a woman is, she has no name.
She walks down the street, never visits the café.

Fatuous nonsense that had never led anywhere, I told myself, women do visit cafés — well, not everywhere, actually, and at their own risk. But then what's so interesting about visiting cafés, I asked myself reproachfully, even scoldingly. Stop blaming your unhappiness on other people! Anyway, you'd have a job describing it. A woman accompanied by a small boy spends the afternoon at the swimming pool — how awful! I gave a snort of mirth, but private snorts of mirth are not a lot of fun.

I inhaled a mouthful of cigarette smoke, studying my aptitude for happiness out of the corner of my mind. But in place of the feeling of peace I had been expecting, I was assailed by a nasty taste. I spat noisily on the floor, attracting hostile, disapproving looks from my neighbours.

Something in the air had made the cigarette taste revolting. I ran to the bar, but neither water nor soda got rid of it. The fact is, all the perfumes of Araby would be incapable of obliterating the taste of Aquaboulevard water. It tasted like bile.

I returned to my place, where the neighbours were now conversing.

'Did you know, the Erjeans have adopted a little black girl.' The speaker was a smart woman wearing a rather silly white headband and 1950s-style make-up with eyeliner around the eyes and huge shadows on the lids. She was perched on the edge of her chair. 'Yes, you know, the family where the uncle died last year on his way home one evening. He was fifty-two. It can come just like that, dying at the wheel of your car. No warning. He was only fifty-two!'

'With everything that's happening in Africa!' replied her companion, an older woman, scratching her leg with a look of total absorption.

'There are Erjeans everywhere,' the first woman went on, 'but they're choice, they really are!'

They both spoke in dense tones specifically designed for our little concrete lounging area, surrounded by shouting, that special swimming-pool sound: laughter, echoes, the lapping of water. I wondered what 'There are Erjeans everywhere' could mean. It had an almost poetic ring.

I ducked back into my book:

> *Full fathom five thy father lies;*
> *Of his bones are coral made;*
> *Those are pearls that were his eyes:*
> *Nothing of him that does fade,*
> *But does suffer a sea-change*
> *Into something rich and strange.*

'Where's Eugenio?' I thought abruptly with a stab of anguish, undoubtedly alerted by Hannah Arendt's message, the obvious allusion to drowning. Yet I knew I must learn to let him be, people told me so every day, almost as if their advice concealed a threat. Yes, I knew I must leave him in peace, even in war sometimes, and be content to listen for which way the wind was blowing without worrying myself sick.

My neighbours were reviewing their acquaintance, good-naturedly amassing solid misfortunes: deaths, injuries, illnesses, whatever.

'We don't go to the country at all any more, you know?' said the woman with the white headband. 'Philippe always hated it so! Well, when the old housekeeper committed suicide I gave up our weekend jaunts to Chenevières. It's OK. At least it saves us those appalling Sunday-evening traffic jams. I come here instead, mainly for the sunbeds and the jacuzzi — and the PE instructor who does the eleven o'clock session.'

I have always admired the gift some people have for organizing a life that presents well, a schedule that always looks good. I should have liked to ask why the housekeeper had committed suicide. I pictured the house in the country, rambler roses smelling of apples, a stretch of grass running down to the river, a mildly deranged gardener who would pounce fiercely on the least little daisy that ruined his lawn and could trim hedges like nobody's business. I pictured the housekeeper, drowned.

'She hadn't been right for some time. Imagine, a foreigner, alone in that village at the back of beyond, no family, nothing, with the rumours there were about her, how the baker had given her a child, which seemed odd because the baker's wife was a much better-looking woman. We'd taken her on because we were sorry for her. Philippe was convinced she raided our pasta store and stole tins of tuna. It never bothered me. We don't exactly have to count the pennies,' the woman with the head-band went on, while the other listened open-mouthed. We both did. 'And to cap it all, no man in the house, and three half-imbecile boys, a constant torment. Her hair was falling out as a result: dreadful for a woman still in her thirties. She'd found some work she could do at home, sealing envelopes for the bank, and then they gave her the sack. She went up into the attic and hanged herself, just like that, no warning, not a word of explanation. There was talk of depression, decompression, something like that.'

Aquaboulevard was stifling me. I ran round the various pools to find Eugenio and his friend. They were jumping up and down inside a kind of lift cabin full of rubber balls, and they looked very pale.

'Come on, we're going!' I shouted through the glass walls of the cage.

Eugenio came out and collapsed at my feet, unconscious.

I threw myself down, patting his cheeks. I was instant-aneously bathed in sweat, the sweat of fear. I covered him with kisses and kept calling his name.

'Don't worry, lady,' his friend said, not looking at all sur-prised, 'I feel sick myself, it's the chlorine, it happens all the time, they say it's set wrong, Eugenio's smaller so it will have affected his system.'

'Quick, fetch me a nurse!' I babbled. But the boy with no

name was right. Eugenio came to, he passed his arms round my neck, smelling horribly of bleach, and he said:

'Shall we go, then?'

'Don't move, the nurse is coming!' I answered.

'No, please not. She'll stick a needle in me!'

He's right, I thought. In the distance, his friend of a day was returning alone.

'It's closed for Christmas,' he explained, 'but you mustn't worry, lady, he might throw up a bit, my little brother did. He just needs to drink some milk. I saw it on television. That's the best thing when you've been poisoned. He'll be right as rain after that.'

I had tears in my eyes. We said goodbye.

'He was very kind, that boy,' I said to Eugenio as we walked away. I might have been trying to recruit a friend for him.

'Oh, mummy, you go all gooey the minute someone talks to you,' Eugenio replied. 'He's just a normal kid, that's all. He's an orphan. That's why he was so nice to you.'

His words struck me forcibly. I've never forgotten them. They implied so many things, some sweet, some disturbing.

'Right, what are we going to eat?' Eugenio went on without a pause.

I waxed lyrical about the food hall at Bon Marché again, making it sound like a kind of Aladdin's cave, the Luna Park of good eating.

'You'll enjoy it, you'll see.'

'Bet I won't,' he said curtly. His gruff tone reminded me of a truth handed down by my mother: the good moments always turn bad at the end. Oddly, though, that alters nothing. In this field, as in every other, experience is no use. It makes you wonder sometimes why we have so pointless a word: *experience*.

I smoked cigarette after cigarette as we walked through the night; they made a little beacon for us. The wet towels soon soaked through the bag, making it slap loudly against my leg with each step.

'I could drop you at the flat if you'd prefer, and go and buy our Christmas Eve meal on my own,' I suggested.

'I don't like being alone at night.'

We arrived in front of the brightly lit department store, a sulk surrounding us like a radioactive cloud.

6

'So how was it, your Christmas Eve?'

The speaker was Clothilde Ouspenski. We were back at work. It was half past nine the next morning, and all the girls looked like marmots who'd been torn from their burrow by an earthquake. I say *girls* because we were all women between thirty and fifty years of age. I don't know why we had adopted the rather silly habit of referring to ourselves in this way. Offices where only women work always have a whiff of boarding-school about them.

Sitting alone in front of her switchboard, demonstrating her usual stubbornness, telephonist Wendy Cope was doing her make-up, as she did every morning. Her equipment was spread out before her. From left to right: foundation, ochre for hollow-ing the cheeks, pink shadow for the cheekbones, powder, mascara, eye-shadow, eye-liner. Nothing on her pale lips. She used to come to work by car, then she'd had time to do it at red lights, but when she got divorced her husband kept the car. She went on making herself up, but on arrival. Wendy had an excellent excuse for not doing it earlier: she had two small daughters, we often talked about them. I liked the warm, humdrum atmosphere of the office in the morning. A cotton wool wadding of silence, which we gradually plucked away with our chatter.

The walls were so thin, in the next room you could hear the sound of envelopes being slit, balls of paper hitting wastepaper baskets. Computers made little peeping noises. There were the ritual tasks: entering new books, filling out cards, indexing. After eleven, the phone began ringing for us to go out and meet people who needed help at the information desk. Afternoons, people would come and read in the reading-room on the ground floor until half-past six. Women, mostly. We had ten tables of light-coloured wood, they made the place look like something between a classroom and a tearoom. Each table was lit by a separate lamp, one with a china base that spread a soft light good for thinking by. I used to love that evening sight, the ten circles of light on the wooden tabletops and the books all spread about, piled up, bristling with paper markers. We mostly got lecturers from the big training establishments, educational sociologists, advisers looking for promotion, students in search of a thesis subject, psycholinguists. And then other, assorted folk, a civil engineer, a metallurgist undergoing retraining, a sports chiropodist, a banker who was expecting a baby and coming to the library was her way of waiting. We saw all sorts. We were called the Education and Childcare Research Library, we had an international reputation, and at the same time this was a place of shelter, a kind of burrow where a creature felt safe from everything, a convent where I'd sought refuge.

We got famous journalists, too. Mireille Dumas came once, afterwards her assistants came in shifts, working up a piece on children who went mad because they were taught to read before the age of two. This was an educational fad (reading before the age of two, not going mad) that emerged in France in the early nineties, launched by Dr. Chapiron and inspired by the enormous success of the books written by the 'super-gifted' Arthur and his parents.

The human mind, particularly the child's mind, is a sumptuous marketplace. In that marketplace, we were one tiny stall.

'Well, I'm staying the way I am!' said Nicole, glaring at Wendy's powder compact. Nicole was our boss, sort of. Whatever she did, wherever in the world, she would have been sort of the boss. She was an expert on the virility myths of American Indian societies and she was not kidding: she really did never wear make-up.

'Painting my face on Christmas Day, which is a public holiday everywhere, that would hurt, that would.'

'Oh, don't exaggerate,' Clothilde said. 'It's for our benefit that they're substituting the 25th for two optional days off. We're way behind with stocktaking, way behind! What I did, I took the 21st, the 22nd, and the 23rd, Saturday, that way we had four days to get ready for Christmas with the kids. You can't have your cake *and* eat it. Plus today my children have gone to their father. That never happens normally!'

She might have been describing a particularly perilous triple backward somersault.

'Right!' said Nicole, half laughing, but in a voice that was slightly tense, edged with anger. 'It's to get it into our brats' heads that we're not housewives and that they owe us respect and support. It's to help us fight for equality between partners that they've robbed us of our Christmas Day! Anyway, I'm off tomorrow and I'm not coming back till next Monday. Clothilde and Nouk, you're minding the shop! I've got some days saved and I'm taking them.'

I listened admiringly, although I detest the word *brat*. We were all feminists at the library, even if we had long since stopped using a word that carries overtones of deadly serious- ness nowadays, possibly even of po-faced gloom. However, there are the strong-minded, and there are the feeble-hearted. The latter irritate the former with their lack of determination, their lack of spirit, their fear of failure, that's the modern term for old-fashioned alienation, 'oppression' we used to call it, grinding poverty the name under which it has always been with us. Oh, it did something for us, reading all these books. We switched vocabularies deftly, the new words becoming our com- panions, shaping the way we thought, and at least, if we made a mess of our lives, we knew whom to blame. But be that as it may, whatever the current syntagm, possibly because of all the linguistic pitching and tossing, it had been a while since I saw things the way Nicole did, so clearly, so trenchantly. Sometimes at night I dreamed of a world divided in two, cowards forming the larger group, fighters the very small one. The small group always won.

'That's all very well!' Clothilde went on. Clothilde adored poring over the tattered fabric of my life. 'But we still don't know how Nouk spent her Christmas Eve!'

'With Eugenio,' I said soberly.

'On his own? You're mad!' Nicole said, pulling her chair over. 'It'll drive the poor lad nuts, all this non-stop intimacy! Was there no one? Your family, your old friends? Christmas, my dear girl, is a collective feast, an ancient rite of passage to help us endure the lack of daylight we all find so deadly, to mark the end of ever-shorter days, to proclaim that life will resume, that deep in the earth the seed is germinating, the harvest invisibly being prepared.'

'Well, we did something new, we had a little party, just the two of us,' I said bravely.

I could have told them about our visit to Bon Marché, where we had arrived around five in the evening.

We found a number of people whom the season had clearly passed by, a row of old men and women who looked as if they had been dumped there, like pets beside summer motorways. Seven or eight of them, sitting as in a day-care centre, either gazing into space or staring at their knees or their walking-sticks. Very small old people, white as sheets and mute as fishes. With tiny toothless mouths and huge hands draped over the tops of walking-sticks.

Eugenio grabbed a trolley and climbed into the child's seat. I should have stopped him, he's too big. We looked a bit ridiculous, and I couldn't have cared less.

'Push me!' he commanded, his bad mood quite forgotten.

We used to love games like that, hurtling down the neatly-stacked aisles. We made a splendid schuss past vegetables and executed several perfect figures of eight round tropical fruits before slaloming between Far-Eastern preserves and English biscuits. There is a geography to supermarkets. It makes them friendly places if you are a regular and hostile if you are a

stranger, just like a village. The supermarket is a logical landscape: it conforms to numerous amusing rules. The rules are
called marketing but they also represent a view of the world,
bristling with innocent booby-traps that reflect the laws of
impulse buying.

Eugenio was always up on the latest novelties that everyone
should have, goodness knows where he got it from. He urged
the trolley on towards the brownies with white almonds, ham
with cherries, fresh lychees, chocolate mousse with whipped
cream, banana and coconut-milk desserts.

'There we are,' he said, 'that's supper. A couple of videos, and
we're in business!' I shivered, wondering what happened to
them later, the little rich kids, when their parents were no
longer rich. Where did they make for, which flock of lemmings
would they join up with?

I felt unable to recount this shameful scene to my colleagues,
nor could I bring myself to tell them about the giant jigsaw-
puzzle exhibition we organized back at the flat. All the jigsaw
puzzles that we owned, some with over fifty pieces, were assem-
bled one by one for the occasion. Afterwards we arranged them
side by side in order of size and difficulty, with titles implying a
secret storyline, price tags to make it all look serious, birth and
death dates, properly hyphenated, and an exhibition catalogue
that took us nearly two hours to put together.

We did not even have time to watch the Lassie video I had
bought in a fit of nostalgia, recalling that striding run and the
incredibly silky coat of the dog with the long nose. I remembered nothing of the story.

It was midnight before we were finished. I was happy and
content, and so was my son. As we sat cross-legged in front of

the exhibition, eating our special ham and our banana and coconut-milk desserts, he said:

'When do our guests arrive?'

My heart missed a beat.

'I don't think they'll be coming this evening,' I said.

I had forgotten one detail: visitors. And our entire dream collapsed. It sounds laughable, I know, but then, many things make us laugh that ought to make us ponder our fecklessness, our want of faith in our own plans. I say 'our' to make myself sound serious, I mean of course 'my'.

'It's too late for anyone to come now,' I told Eugenio, dry-mouthed. 'Anyway, it's time for bed. Tomorrow, when you wake up, your presents will be under the tree.'

'What a hopeless Christmas! I should have gone away to holiday camp,' my son said then and went off dragging his feet, not giving me a kiss. That was why, next morning, my eyes were swollen. I did not feel like boasting of my achievements.

'Well,' said Nicole, 'my men gave me a fabulous evening!' And we all closed our ears, not wishing to hear any more. Nicole's silk négligées and champagne flutes, the love of her four sons, huge smooth-skinned fellows with extravagant eyebrows, the exquisite submissiveness of her husband who adored her and who, better than anyone, protected her from herself, the ardour of her lover: we knew the whole story by heart, and it was not one of our favourites. We often suspected that Nicole's main purpose in living it was to be able to narrate it to us, because it must have been a hard life, attracting so much envy.

'Don't you find it sillier and sillier, this swapping presents at

Christmas?' Clothilde observed dreamily. 'I call it the great unwanted-present fair. I even have a special cupboard where we put the pathetic relics of our misunderstandings. The scratchy sweaters, the boring records, the novelty socks, the ghastly paperweights, the everlasting snowballs, the awful pictures, the fake jewellery, the salad bowls, the writing sets, the mock-leather handbags, the diaries.'

'Stop it, *please!*' I begged, tears in my eyes, seeing once again the gift I had found under the Christmas tree that morning, that year's diary entirely revised by my son, with the date corrected on each page and a little note saying: 'You will use this, won't you?'

'You're right, Clothilde,' I quietly agreed, 'you're always right, but we're not made of stone, and even shut away in a cupboard, presents never stop hurting, presents received as well as presents not received, the countless presents that were just wrong, the presents that misfired, the presents that cost too much and felt like blackmail or were received in that spirit, and the presents we've all of us left behind in the house of the giver. They're like an army of inexorable insects, determined to drag us down, and worst of all are the ones we leave behind on purpose: the presents that, though chosen with love, give no pleasure.'

'You can be a real pain when you try,' Nicole remarked. 'You should find a street corner to preach on, get it off your chest!' And she went back to her office to write a paper on the initiation rites of male over-eights in a Hopi tribe to which she is particularly attached.

Clothilde attacked her post. We talked of her 'ministerial in-tray'. The fact was, she wrote masses of letters and got none back. The opposite of ministers. Every morning Clothilde pounced on the post-bag that Wendy was quietly sorting. She would scrabble through the piles of letters, making us laugh because she was like a little dog then, looking for the bone it has buried. She used to write the kind of letter she'd have liked to receive. Don't we all, though, aren't we all the same, and what good does it do us?

My job was reading. I would read everything that came in and then write a piece about it, which appeared in the specialist journal that covered our field. I also had to report on the various 'fairs' that were becoming ever more popular; the regional Educational Book Fairs, the Parents' Fair, the Grandparents' Fair, the Family Holidays Fair, the Au Pair Girls' Fair, the new cross-curricular colleges springing up at the rate of a dozen a week. So I was a regular visitor to the exhibition halls at the Porte de Versailles as well as to various prefabricated buildings in provincial cities, where, jostled by crowds that the organizers no doubt found reassuring and that boded well for the future of education, I had thrust upon me thousands of brochures written in identical jargonese and printed in identical colours. These I would describe, trying to keep a straight face (not always easy) and assessing their contribution to the sum total of human knowledge. The Education Library was, after all, a primarily scientific institution.

I went to my desk and switched on the little portable radio that I kept permanently tuned to the music programme. I put the paper cup of boiling coffee down on the white envelope placed there for the purpose, which I would throw away as soon as the number of brown rings became greater than I could stand. I took out a cigarette. I surveyed with satisfaction my little piles of coloured cards, my Apple Mac set artistically at an angle, my Breton ceramic pot of pens, my stack of books arranged in order of size rather than date of arrival, my vase with its single flower, my lead hedgehog sculpture. Every office is a coded portrait of one kind or another, sending a message to the world with its meticulous, absurd order, its cosy charm. Mine set me thinking about prison cells, lorry-drivers' cabs. Quarter past eleven. I wondered whether to ring Eugenio and wake him. I stopped myself doing so. I opened a book: Marie-France Bach, *Feasting and Failing*. Stimulated by the title, I threw myself into the text with that curious hope cultivated, I suppose, by others as well as myself: that one day we shall find, in a book, THE answer to a question about which we have not the faintest idea, a sort of universal solution, explanation and solace. In fact, it was a pretty woolly commercial operation, and if the book had arrived too late to find a small place in the wounded hearts of all enemies of Christmas, that was no great loss. It discussed the festivals of Dionysus and Bacchus and their modern equivalents. It was a learned tome, lamentably devoid of the wit implicit in the title.

'What shall we put down as subject-areas?' Wendy asked. Wendy looks after the catalogue as well as the telephone. I had my answer ready:

'Soap, nettles, breast-feeding, spiders, formalin.'

One thing I enjoyed doing was identifying subject-areas before reading the book. It was a knack one picked up.

Sometimes, when she had a moment, Wendy would ask me to justify my entries. I loved doing that.

We had a lot of fun dreaming up subject-areas, Wendy and I. Curiously, no one ever complained. There were only two possible explanations: either no one ever consulted the catalogue seriously, or people believed us and in thirty years' time we should have revolutionized taxonomy. Wendy, as well as being a switchboard operator, had written a large number of marvellous poems, delicate, funny and deeply moving. I could quote some here, but they ought to be printed all together: they set one another off, rather like a field of young rabbits. They're modern, subversive poems, telling of the pleasures of breakfast-time, the sweetness of men's sleep, so much better than ours, the demerits of rain, the war of the sexes, the little prayers one needs to devise if one is to have any chance of staying out of trouble.

Between twelve and one we often went out for a hard-boiled egg in a dimly-lit café where the people were friendly and the seats covered with green imitation leather. I used to drink beef tea, Wendy China tea, and we dunked our eggs like biscuits as we discussed our recent reading and laughed over things that made us cry. Between us, we discovered a host of little laws of everyday life that no one ever talked about. Why were we so low in the morning? What made us so tired? Why, sometimes, did we not have the faintest idea what to cook for supper that evening? And why did we have access to no other feeling than that of being a prisoner (but of what?) or an escapee (but from what?)?

I often talked about Hannah Arendt, whose phrase 'the barbed evasions of the heart' had impressed me so much. It seemed to account for so many hurts. Wendy thought it would make a good motto for a Valentine card. Too cynical for my taste.

Our little talks used to cheer us up, and Wendy sometimes wrote poems about them, which she would then wrap in Japanese paper like crumpled silk and leave on my desk, knowing how much I adored surprises.

Sometimes, Nicole and Clothilde dropped into the same café for a beer or a coffee. I remember Clothilde once reading us a letter she had written to a pop star. The fiftieth — which he would not answer any more than he had the others. Nicole left to make a private phone call and returned with pink cheeks and a ladder in her stocking. She did it just to annoy us. I wondered how she managed the laddered stocking. And why it made me faintly jealous.

Together, or separately, they would stuff us with depressing advice, give us a good ticking-off.

'Contrary to what you might believe, you're a couple of whining bitches who are scared of life, you aren't poets at all!' Nicole told me one day when I had particularly exasperated her. Later I told Wendy, who merely shrugged.

'Whining bitches, poets: two sides of the same coin!' she said wisely. 'It's a bit like femme fatale and vamp. You'll see, when you're famous again, she'll talk differently to you then! She'll even have forgotten what she thought before.'

Wendy's optimism was the most moving aspect of her flayed-cat personality.

That day, while I was reading *Feasting and Failing*, chapter eight, page 132 ('Anniversaries serve only the enemy'), dozing intermittently because I had understood nothing for the last twenty or thirty pages, Nicole came in and sat down opposite me.

'You're in a bad way, girl!' she pointed out, not unkindly. 'So look, I've brought you something that should help.'

At the library, apart from her research into Hopi children and

their acrobatic but proven techniques for passing into adult-
hood, Nicole was responsible for those specialist journals that
proliferate on our news-stands like thistles across the countryside. She would cart them around from room to room, reading
extracts aloud to us, never letting us laugh. She was in charge of
classifying them, by series but also by content and subject-area,
which meant we had to have several copies. Nicole would cut
out articles, paste them onto sheets of cheap coloured card
(beige or orange) and arrange them in files.

This was no easy task, because the journals were all much the
same and so were the articles: indigestible scientific reports set
in tiny type inside little grey or green borders, the sole purpose
of which was to make them look serious, adorned with huge
colour photographs and interspersed with advice, following the
fashion of the day, about school work, wearing spectacles during puberty, orthopaedic soles, learning foreign languages,
choosing the right bed, harmless tranquillizers, baby-sitters,
headaches in the refractory child, tummyache in the submissive
child, the number of eggs it is advisable to consume per week,
choosing a bicycle, dental appliances, the best time to conceive
a second child without disturbing the first, natural sources of
phosphorous, the best time to conceive a fifth child without
disturbing the other four, the role of the modern father, classi-
cal dance for small boys with a history of violence, the little-known
risks of rectal temperature checks, the best sea-water cures for
children, the new role of the uncle in the fragmented mono-
nuclear family, adolescents and the end of identity crises, the
place of pottery in teaching maths, vitamin A and curvature of
the spine, schoolbags, the rights and wrongs of catechization,
hairdressers for children, the authority of in-laws, relationships

within the clan as the ultimate model of the conjugal relationship, compression of the spinal column in under-fours, short
hairy legs, these were just some of the subjects, along with a
hundred thousand others, to receive weekly or monthly attention in a plethora of publications in the field of education and
childcare. Nicole took her work very seriously, seeing such
journals as a key element in the democratization of medical
knowledge. Her own words.

'What's the news from the happy families front, then?' I
asked. Quite innocently, it seemed to me.

Whenever I made fun of the advice she was always dishing
out about how to get rid of cellulite, or wrinkles, or cholesterol,
or general maternal anguish, her usual reply was a laughing
suggestion that a few subscriptions would do me no harm.

But this time I could see she was livid.

'If you take people for idiots, that's your loss! Reading articles
about health and education never hurt anyone. Quite the opposite, actually. Besides, research has shown that people don't go
straight out and buy the new products hyped by the journals,
nor do parents put their children on a low-sodium diet the
instant they read an article extolling the benefits of one!'

'You mean they wait for others to act as guinea-pigs?'

She had risen to her feet and was pacing back and forth in
front of my desk. A fold of her clouded-alpaca poncho knocked
over my vase, her bosom strained at the poncho's plunging
neckline, she snatched up my hedgehog and began tossing it in
her palm, her voice rose. She was furious and hurt, as if she
herself had been the editor-in-chief of one of those rags.

'They simply like having these things discussed. It's like
cruises, it costs nothing to leaf through a magazine and fanta-

size about going on a cruise. Will you never understand? People need to dream! Poking fun at things one knows nothing about is hardly indicative of an enquiring mind!' she snapped, exhausted.

'Nor does spouting a string of platitudes scribbled by squalid journalists in the pay of drug companies and medical hotel chains!' I replied pleasantly.

Some days, the euphemisms that are inseparable from office life, no doubt created for office life, simply elude one, leaving only real words.

I glanced at the magazine Nicole was waving at me: *Happiness Plus*.

'Even the titles are over the top,' I said. 'That one sounds like the work of a bad satirical science-fiction writer.' And in an attempt to get her on my side:

'Have you got the latest *Aspects of Woman*? The advertising campaign is …' (I often dispensed with epithets, letting my intonation suffice.) 'I'd like to see *that*!'

The campaign featured a picture of three women with masses of teeth, peering skyward in a sporty, ecstatic fashion in the midst of a greeny-blue landscape. Maybe there was a forest in the background, I had forgotten. What I did remember was thinking that the people who create such images have all the luck, getting to visit such beautiful places. It might have been an ad for a new sanitary towel.

'Just stop believing you're stronger than everyone else!' Nicole replied in a gruff but kindly way. 'Look, this is what I've brought you.'

In the centre of the magazine, just after an article with the splendid title 'What our children do with their money', commissioned by a major high-street bank and devoted to the squirreling impulses of children aged between nine and thirteen and the millions of francs set aside as a result, there was a double-page spread headlined:

ANXIOUS? DESPERATE? IRRITABLE?
AT LAST — A SOLUTION!

I looked up.
'Is it that bad, do you reckon?'
'It made me think of you, that's all.'
'Thanks a lot.'
I went back to *Feasting and Failing*, page 144, chapter heading: 'Those who know where to place themselves'. It may seem esoteric, but it was all about working out when, and in what circumstances, children learn to locate themselves geographically within a festive space, i.e. a large room full of other kids, plastic cups of Coca-Cola and plates of cakes, surrounded by a din that is half playground and half cocktail party, with the added hazard of the confetti and the wads of discarded chewing-gum that stick to the shoes of the same people all their lives without anyone knowing why fate particularly has it in for them right from the age of five, probably up until the day they die.
'Right, I'll be off, then,' Nicole said. 'And don't forget: you need to take a couple of days' holiday. I'm starting mine tomorrow.'
I began to read the article.
This was the method pioneered by Dr. Wolfli: *Wildflowers, Elixirs and Thornbushes.*

Poetry, but a poetry that I could smell coming, although I could not describe it: a kind of poisoned poetry.

I glossed over the preliminaries (which bristled with capital letters: Peace, Harmony, Strength, Vital Energy) to get at the summary of the states of being that Nicole had recognized in me and that Dr. Wolfli proposed to remedy. Forty-eight plants and floral compositions were listed, thanks to which, ever since some far-off time peopled by billhook-wielding Druids, men had been able, if they so desired, to cure the ills of the soul. I read:

> For anxiety, the feeling of being under threat without being able to tell why, Aspen.
> For fear of the dark, of tomorrow, and of others' illnesses, Nutmeg.
> For utter despair, prostration with no prospect but emptiness, Sweet Chestnut.
> For the person who never thinks he or she is doing well enough and feels responsible for others' mistakes, Norway pine.
> For protection against the influence of events and to help break ties, Walnut.
> For excessive concern for the well-being of other people, particularly relatives, together with fear of the worst, Red Chestnut.

I felt like laughing. 'Won't be a big demand for Red Chestnut,' I muttered privately. 'Can't see anyone suffering from that kind of ailment, excessive concern for others, ho ho ho!'

At that precise moment the telephone rang, and I knew: the gods had taken their revenge. I dreaded some disaster. A thunderbolt from an enraged Dr. Wolfli.

'Hello, mummy,' came my son's trembly little voice.

'All right, darling? Have you woken up?' I answered stupidly. My palms felt sweaty.

'Do you know what's happened?' he asked in a doom-laden voice.

Fires, floods, turned ankles from jumping out of bed, maniacs with crazed imaginations, oh leave me alone, I prayed.

'It's the Queen. They've just said on TV: she's lost the keys to Windsor Castle. Have you heard?'

Eugenio was speaking in a whisper, very fast, with deep feeling. 'Is it serious, do you think? Maybe she won't be able to get into her home?'

Poor Elizabeth, I thought, hat awry, banging on the big door, breaking a nail, and no one comes: the castle is empty. She stands alone on her own doormat.

'Don't worry,' I said, 'queens are never alone. Nor do they have doormats.'

'What was that, mummy?'

As I talked, my eye roamed over Dr. Wolfli's article: *Elm, for someone who does not feel up to the task in hand.*

Might try some of that, I thought. I asked Eugenio the ritual questions, the sugary, embarrassing questions that mothers ask over the phone. I told him I should be home soon.

'The thing is, mummy, I'm bored,' he said. 'I'm bored, mummy,' he repeated. I wanted to hang up.

'Watch a film! There's a brilliant documentary about the love-life of the penguin. I put it on the shelf by the window. I recorded that for you. You'll see, the time will fly by.'

He said: 'I've gone off penguins. They scare me. Anyway, if penguins stopped breeding, no one would have a problem. But don't worry, mummy, I'll be all right. I'll go and see Adam.'

I went back to my book and began writing my abstract of *Feasting and Failing*, five lines per chapter, based on the notes I had jotted down as I read. I had already forgotten Adam's existence, I realized.

Wendy came in. Wendy is so sensitive that a change of mood in the office has for her the intensity of a change in the weather for anyone else. 'Do you know the true story of the librarian who thought she'd finally found a way of bringing in readers?' she asked sweetly.

I looked up and became aware that two tears of anxiety were running down my cheeks. They were what had drawn Wendy to me.

'I really must get some glasses. A librarian from where was that?' I replied, embarrassed.

The phone rang again. Wendy answered it, then passed me the receiver:

'It's Martha,' she said, wrinkling her nose.

She disliked Martha. 'Those nymphomaniac prison warders you surround yourself with! I don't know where you dig them up!' she'd told me one day, blushing angrily. Such violence, coupled with such vulgarity, had touched me.

'It's Martha, she's calling from Brittany.'

'You're coming, then!' said a firm but excited voice. It was not a question. 'I've booked your tickets, you've only to pick them up at the station. You're catching the three o'clock train this afternoon. We'll meet you at the barrier. The weather's lovely, and the whole family's looking forward to seeing you.' Wendy shrugged.

I said: 'We will, we'll come! It's so good of you to bother.' I fell over myself, thanking her. I said: 'How wonderful to have real friends!'

Wendy shifted in her seat indiscreetly. Martha's voice, as usual, was audible several feet from the receiver.

Shaking off a slight sitcom feeling that had come over me, I hung up with: 'See you soon, darling, thank you so much!' and went in to see Nicole. She took care of our days off.

I told her I was going away. I told her I had been thinking, and I thanked her for Dr. Wolfli's spiritual herbarium.

Nicole hugged me. I could see she was happy to have had such an influence on things, on my life. I thought: she's proud to be an example, I'm a worm, I'm less than nothing.

We went back to work, because I still had to finish the morning.

'Tell me the rest of your librarian story,' I asked Wendy innocently. She gave me a rather scornful look.

Wendy pulled her huge witch-mohair cardigan more tightly round her. 'Don't you find it cold?' she asked accusingly.

'Are you going anywhere for New Year?'

'Boris is taking me to Prague. Four whole days. I think that's why I feel cold all the time. I'm cold because I'm afraid. Afraid of the cold, especially.' I gave her a friendly smile. 'We'll be on a train for sixteen hours. It'll be our honeymoon. The children are staying with my mother. Philippe refused to have them, he said he's certainly not doing anything to —'

She laughed suddenly. It made her bird-like. I had forgotten all about Philippe, her ex-husband. She said: 'I feel ashamed whenever I say his name nowadays, even in the most banal contexts. Every sentence I utter comes out loaded with innuendo. That's how I can tell my life is such a mess. Divorce stories are so disgusting, don't you find? I hear the words spewing out of my mouth and I can't believe them. Such horrible things, such obscene thoughts, how is it we all dance to this tune?'

I was grateful to her for saying such things.

'Will you tell me about it? Perhaps you'll give me a ring? And do tell me quickly your story about the librarian, I must go soon, Eugenio goes crazy on his own. I don't feel easy in my mind.'

'When do you ever feel easy in your mind, Nouk?'

Wendy's eyes were all screwed up with love for me.

'Six feet under, you'll still find something to worry about: the wood the coffin was made of, the quality of the soil, what kind of worms are present.'

'Thank you for thinking of that,' I said sharply. I'm not too fond of such scene-setting.

She pulled her black cardigan tight again, almost as if she were trying to stretch the wool twice round her body. She rubbed her arms.

'The librarian (she was a little Arkansas lady, I believe) was annoyed that no one came in to borrow books. The library was a large, light building, full of books, all neatly arranged. What should she do? So she composed a small ad for insertion in the local newspaper: *A hundred-dollar bill has inadvertently been left in a library book. If the reader who finds it will kindly return it to us, he or she will receive a reward.* I think she thought, poor thing, that people needed only to come to the library, needed only to have a book in their hands, and they would start to read.

'Next morning, people turned up. By lunchtime, the library was a shambles. Shelves had been toppled over, torn books littered the aisles. No stone left unturned, so to speak. And of course no one had read any more than before.'

I thought: No, they hated books, didn't they? Books were, without exception, a snare and a delusion!

'I'd have preferred it if there had been a bill,' I said softly to Wendy.

'I really like that story,' Wendy said as she gave me an affectionate goodbye kiss. 'There are so many conclusions one can draw from it! Wish me a good trip, then. See you Monday week!'

7

Leaving the office, I started to run. A clock struck midday. Ignoring the 'Do not walk on the grass' sign, I crossed the threadbare patch of green in the middle of the square. It was sprinkled with little white dots. Snowdrops already, I whispered wonderingly, my heart skipping a beat as an idiotic wave of pleasure swept through me. I slowed down to pick one, thinking: Eugenio will be so pleased, he loves flowers. I winced as I stooped. Idiot. Why imagine snowdrops in December, even if the seasons are all wrong now, even if our ozone layer is getting increasingly holey? Yes, why would there be snowdrops? To take the edge off our massacre of nature? My mind was suddenly awash with all the things we vaguely reiterate, like talking sheep, all the things we stir into one enormous fear, which is at the same time a laziness, and which can be summed up in two words: 'Take cover!' The lawn in the square was littered with tiny feathers, white down. Probably a couple of seagulls fighting, I scolded myself, looking vaguely around for a corpse. Why is it that small white feathers produce such an effect? Their lightness, I suppose, makes them a symbol of the vulnerability of existence: no sooner shed than dispersed. They certainly do last well, you find them weeks later, caught on a twig here, a bush there.

I ran down into the metro: the train was in, restoring my faith in my star. I took a seat, still talking to myself, humming to keep my spirits up, trying to stop myself trembling. Rattling through my head, going faster and faster, was a list of things to do: stop at the dry-cleaner's, pack the bags, call in at the chemist. Was there still a decent suitcase in the flat? I remembered, once upon a time, never leaving for a journey without sending the trunks on ahead, the one trunk to be precise, a splendid object, incredibly capacious, just the job for well-ironed linen. Why, oh why had I accepted the invitation?

We were so numbed, Eugenio and I, every jolt was a threat.

I looked up, there was a couple sitting opposite. They could not see me. They were very old. He was tiny, with a head of fluffy white hair, round spectacles, large, almost implausibly large ears, big nose with hair sprouting from the nostrils, neat, clearly defined mouth, cleft chin, velvet waistcoat. He was holding a stick with a duck's-head handle, and his two hands were laid carefully one on top of the other, flat on the head of the bird. The woman was wrapped in a fur coat.

After rummaging in an enormous sealskin bag with plastic handles, she produced two large sweets, one orange and one yellow. She peeled the paper off the orange one and gave it to her lover to suck. The sugary ball could be seen passing from one thin cheek to the other. I wondered whether to envy them or speculate meanly on the sinister slavery, the pathetic dominance that every relationship breeds. We never get beyond the bottle-feeding stage, that's the ghastly truth, I told myself, forgetting for a moment the hellish prospect of packing.

As I watched, the woman smiled at me. She peeled the large yellow sweet and held it out to me, saying something in Russian. I can never refuse that kind of thing. I am as polite as I am phobic and, with a prayer that the germs would spare me, trying to remember the illnesses one can pick up, accepting sweets from strangers, I popped the sweet in my mouth, thinking that in fact I preferred the red ones. So did she, because she took out a third sweet, a lovely poppy-red, which she then stripped of its wrapping. And there we sat, the three of us, sucking away at our boiled sweets.

I combed the depths of memory for a few friendly words to say in Russian, *xorocho, spassiba, dasvidania,* then I got off the train.

Daniel's the dry-cleaner was a landmark in our quarter. It was a very old business with 'Traditional Laundry' written across the front in large italic lettering painted in white on a wine-coloured background. The smell of starch almost reached the street, and the inside of the shop always sent me into a day-dream. There was the noise of the huge machines revolving, and washing could be seen leaping about behind the glass, the water swirling and making waves. Any minute one expected a face to appear, or a plastic duck, a little mermaid, possibly a fish. From racks suspended from the ceiling hung dozens of evening gowns in percale and silk, first-communion dresses, plain-looking bodices, collars of drawn-thread work, lace trimmings, blouses that went with the kinds of bra women used to wear, all theatrical. And there were fairy costumes and shelves with hundreds and hundreds of shirts buttoned around a cardboard collar insert. One wondered if anyone ever came to collect them.

Daniel's was on my route, and I often dropped off my favourite dress in the morning.

'For dry-cleaning, to pick up this evening, please, Mademoiselle Metaxas!'

The smell of warm woollen material, over-ironed with the ironing-machine before being wrapped up, always gave me the impression that I was being well looked after, and I adored Angélique Metaxas. The first time I took my dress in she smiled at me, gave me a searching look and said: 'Good luck, my dear!', sketching a rapid gesture, some kind of Eastern blessing, I assumed. As if she knew everything, and with such warmth that I have never forgotten it.

I often stopped to chat, and she told me all about the disasters that had befallen her family, a large Greek family driven from the country by the democratic revolution led by Venizélos in 1917. White Greeks, so to speak, she would say with a laugh. They went from country to country without paying too much attention to what was happening where they settled, they were not in the habit of bothering about other people, taking circumstances into account, battling with reality. They remained locked in their dream. And before long in their bitterness. Very soon, their money ran out. None of them had ever worked. As for the grand-children, they'd had no choice: taxi-drivers, head waiters, or a job in dry-cleaning because of a Cypriot cousin who owned a chain. Mademoiselle Metaxas would have liked to be a singer.

'I had a voice like a diva, people were always telling me, but I

should have had to take lessons, *efkaristo poli*! It's terrible for
the voice, this business, terrible!' she would often say with a
sigh.

She still had a regal manner. When she said 'a voice like a
diva', I imagined her on-stage, the velvet curtain raised for a
final bow to tiers of gilded, garlanded balconies. Women, drip-
ping with diamonds and flourishing opera-glasses and fans,
leaned forward, cooing. Angélique, in her filmy stage attire,
threw an embrace around the whole world, enveloping it in
yearning melody. Actually, it was a sort of Édith Piaf that I
heard, but I dressed her like La Castafiore, remembering the
days when I designed costumes and painted sets. I used to think
it was lucky Mademoiselle Metaxas would never know.

That day she was feeling sorry for herself, she was getting hot
flushes.

'Can you imagine, in this weather! What a dreadful invention
snow is, typically modern. It looks clean but is disgusting! And
how awful it is, having rivers of cold sweat run down your spine!
My mother never told me about this. Or else I wasn't listening.
I have red cheeks all day and I can't bear it, being cold and then
hot in the shop here. Growing old is truly odious, *boje moï*.'

I used to pop in and see Angélique Metaxas almost every day.
She gave me ridiculous advice because her outlook on life was
totally useless. She would tell me details about the ruination of
her family. I used to get hopelessly lost because she forgot key
moments, mangled people's names, omitted dates. When I
asked questions, she would say plaintively: 'How am I to remember
things that happened so long ago, why should I remember
things that give me so little pleasure, and what good is it all to
you, my pretty one, what could you ever learn from this humdrum

mish-mash? People whirling around the world like dervishes, usually from east to west, yes, give or take a handful, idiot Russians, cretinous Jews, fools of Spaniards, uncouth Turks, awkward Armenians, gypsies, Romanians, people all over the place, no knowing who's who any more, Constantinople, Alexandria, always the same stories: triumphs, daggers, parties, gambling debts, imminent persecutions, predictable betrayals, the same story everywhere, people hacked to pieces, seized, loaded in the same old lorries, thrown behind the same old barbed wire. I often wonder where it comes from, all those millions of kilometres of barbed wire, who manufactures it, who supplies it, because it's everywhere, and it's always the same, you look some time, my God, how nothing changes, and at the end of it all the communal grave, the concealed bodies, the thickets where the deed had been done, usually, and then, too, the fine damask cloths, shrouds, gone are the heavy sheets that were once handed down from mother to daughter, those of birth and those of death, whoops, hurried departures made people forget everything, jewellery hidden in loaves of bread, beautiful girls with big black eyes weeping, eyes you could drown in, oh, forget it, I'd rather forget the whole useless hotchpotch, here, take my nightmares, anyone who wants them! How I hate them often, the ones who doctor memories, academics with their dreamless nights. Only people who have nothing to forget want others to remember.'

I listened open-mouthed, drinking in her words, swallowing the bait. It was odd, her imprecations soothed something in me. Angélique Metaxas possessed the spirit of contradiction that is the mark of the true poet. You hardly expected to hear the truth from her. She didn't give a fig for the truth, didn't believe in it. I often wondered why she had never married. Eugenio liked her too, she used to tell him stories about the British queen, whom her grandmother had known well, apparently, at Windsor Castle or Buckingham Palace, the queen before, of course, poor woman. If she could see what was happening now, princesses in short skirts and probably poor-quality material at that, and the outboard motorboats on which they had themselves photographed. It was all so vulgar. Mademoiselle Metaxas nourished a particular hatred for the outboard motorboat. I doubt whether she had ever seen one outside a glossy magazine. For her, monarchy was the only form of government, and she had little photographs of Queen Sophie, the Danish queen, Margrete II, and King Bhumibol of Thailand. She feared for them. She knew that the outboard motorboat, and all that went with it, would be the death of her fragile idols. She was more afraid of the outboard motorboat than of the masses, whom she had joined without realizing it, and about whose republicanism she had her doubts. I never discussed my ancestors with her, nor did she ever enquire.

That day, as I pushed open the door of Daniel's the dry-cleaner, I prayed that my black woollen dress would be ready. Its plunging back was just the thing for New Year's Eve. A girl I had seen a couple of times before asked to see my ticket.

Where was Mademoiselle Metaxas? A strange anxiety gripped me. I hardly dared ask. You don't do that sort of thing in Paris, it is indiscreet.

'Where is Mademoiselle Metaxas?' I asked the girl.

'Gone. We've seen the back of her.'

'She's not sick?'

'Oh no,' the girl laughed, 'we're the ones who are sick.'

'You wouldn't know where I could write to her?'

A man emerged from behind the machines. He was the girl's father. They resembled each other the way fathers and daughters do sometimes, extremely. I thought: resemblances both amuse and disturb us because they remind us that we are poor creatures, distant cousins of the rabbit. We decide nothing.

In its cage by the door, a mynah bird started jabbering: 'You're blind, mate, you're blind, mate!' Or possibly it was about ironing: 'Ain't ironed right, ain't ironed right!' That was what I thought, anyway, the bird spoke rather indistinctly.

The man was perspiring, he had ugly sweat-stains under his armpits. He said: 'What was it you wanted Mademoiselle Metaxas for?' He made the name sound like a gob of spit. He'd seen too many westerns, so had I.

I hesitated.

'Nothing,' I said, 'nothing. I was just surprised, you know, she'd been here so long. It doesn't matter, honestly, I'll call again.' The words bounced about nonsensically. You stupid mynah bird, I told myself. I upset my purse picking up the dress. I wanted to be off.

'She was stealing money, if you must know,' the man said savagely, heaving a sigh at the same time as if in a bid for sympathy. 'I mean to say, someone you've trusted, she'd had her fingers in the till for years, I don't know how much she's set me back, and now when I press charges she vanishes, curse it, her with her lousy menopause et cetera et cetera, all the yarns she span, all lies, a mythomaniac, a thief and a mythomaniac, filthy bitch, should have her ovaries ripped out, you don't know the half of it.'

I had the absurd impression that he was staring at my stomach.

I ran home sobbing. Never would I go back to Daniel's, I resolved, she was quite right to help herself from that fat bastard's till, I bet she didn't take enough. She could never have taken enough to make up for those hot flushes, those insults, all her other disappointments. I mouthed her so innocent-sounding first name over and over again: Angélique, Angélique.

Eugenio was waiting for me on the landing, he looked down as I climbed the stairs, he took me by the hand, very pleased with himself: he had taken out all the suitcases and laid them open on the big bed.

'See, I've got everything ready!'

Whenever it came to leaving, I felt giddy. An emptiness, whoops, here we go again.

'Do you think there'll be little lamps on the train?'

I liked them too, the little lamps you got on trains. I forgot we should be travelling by day, I was in a dream, we threw in sweaters, socks, pyjamas, God knows what else, and that was it, two cases were ready, packing takes no time when you include almost everything.

'Pity we're not going by plane,' I said as I slammed the street door behind us, having first given a friendly wave to Adam, who seemed to have settled down perfectly with his new brothers and was singing better than ever, seemingly without a scrap of remorse for anything whatsoever. 'I could have shown you the rabbits in Roissy airfield.'

That made him laugh.

'Mummy, you're the one who's wild about rabbits. I prefer trains. And when I told them at school what you'd said about man being descended not just from monkeys but also, maybe even more so, from rabbits, everyone teased me so much that I'm sure it's not true.'

I said nothing, albeit disappointed by such weak-mindedness. It was so blindingly obvious to me that man was descended from the rabbit! Oh Galileo, I sighed, how nothing changes, nothing at all, indeed you died in vain!

But the road climbed, and the wind was icy. We walked quickly, lugging our cases. The station came in sight. In the middle of the concourse stood an old-fashioned merry-go-round, vast and deserted.

'Just one go,' Eugenio begged.

I protested: 'Oh really, you're not an infant any more!'

I felt a great wave of nostalgia. Thousands of goes on merry-go-rounds jostled in my memory, it was always cold, I remembered, there was always a wind whipping round the wooden horses, the one in the Square Boucicaut, almost shabby-looking, the earth around it usually churned to mud, the one in the Rue de Rivoli, huge, gold-painted horses two metres high, the one in the Luxembourg Gardens with its rings that you threaded on a metal rod, just lifting your bottom off the saddle. I used to enjoy climbing on merry-go-rounds with Eugenio when he was one or two. The man in charge would let me, even though it was forbidden. It was like introducing Eugenio to adventure, initiating him into life. Concentrate now, I told myself. Tickets, booking-office, the familiar feeling of being at fault, late, frightened, all so familiar. I pulled out the crumpled piece of paper on which I had scrawled the code Martha dictated. I read it. What a farce, I thought, all those numbers.

'PQ9T865MI72? Here are your tickets, ma'am,' the young

man said. 'One child and one adult, Paris-Brest, two second-class non-smoking windows.'

I thought of the little lamps.

'Would you have two spare first-class seats?'

That made the boy laugh.

'If there are spare seconds, there'll always be spare firsts, but it's almost twice as much!' He looked as if he disapproved of such habits, particularly where a child was concerned.

The compartment was splendid, grey with little orange lamps. We were exultant, Eugenio and I, the moment of climbing into our carriage would stay with us for ever, I knew. We opened up like imperial flowers, one large orchid and one small one. We laid out our things around us, our magazines, our onion-flavoured crisps, our eucalyptus pastilles. Every trip is implicit in the instant of departure.

Whenever Alfonso, back when we were in love, used to say: 'Come out and join me, come and join me in America, come and join me in China, come and join me in Tangiers, in Montpellier ...' my heart would sink, tears sprang to my eyes, a little of my love died each time. One day I simply had to tell him: It's joining you I don't like. There's never anyone there when I arrive, just a little note on a bed or table: 'Back soon.' What I like, I told him, is leaving together, calling a taxi together, half-running down the platform, heart racing, counting off the numbers of the carriages, spotting in the distance the little orange light of the compartment.

Almost imperceptibly, the train moved away from the platform.

'Now no one can bother us!' I said defiantly.

Eugenio was not listening, completely absorbed by the sound.

It made me think of when I was a child and train windows opened, and how at the moment of departure we used to lean out of the lowered window to wave, sometimes even holding mother's hand as she ran alongside, running as far and keeping us company for as long as she could. The engine soon defeated her, though. Afterwards, for a long time we would watch the telegraph posts flit by, and the rails run out behind us as we rounded a curve, and the countryside gradually establish itself, trees and stretches of water, lines of poplars like sums in an exercise-book. But before long we had to duck back in because of the bits of burning grit that injured many a child's eye. Eugenio seemed to have abandoned himself to the marvellous sound of the train, which made me think of how the world was gently closing up behind us. Goodbye world, I thought. A train, like a ship at sea, is a shield against everything.

'I'm bored, mummy, I'm bored,' Eugenio announced, and I looked at him fearfully. 'Will we be there soon?'

'In three hours,' I said. 'Three hours less five minutes, look at those cows, aren't they funny? They must be so cold, the grass is all white. Two hours and fifty minutes,' I said. I always forgot how time tended to get stuck.

'Shall I show you how to turn quarters of an hour into minutes?'

Eugenio gave me a look of deep disgust. The kind that came over him whenever I suggested spelling games, a few conjugations for fun, all those tricks that children can spot a mile off, the leer that goes with the 'Hey, what about revising a times table?'

'They said we shouldn't work during the holidays. When dad rang, when you were at the office, he said: "Your mother really shouldn't leave you on your own on a day like this." And: "I hope she's not making you work too hard, tell her to give you a breather occasionally like everyone else".'

My heart stood still. I was looking at him, and for a second he was not my son. He frightened me.

'What would you like to do, then?' I felt pathetic, at his mercy, a coward, crushed.

'I'd like to play cards. But we don't have a pack.'

Energy surged back. When it came to improvising, I was all ideas. Simple: we must make one.

We spread sheets of paper on our little folding tables, we had to cut them up into thirty-two equal oblongs, that was all. Eugenio wanted to play poker, and for poker a pack of thirty-two cards would do. He took care of hearts and clubs. I did spades and diamonds.

Just past Rennes, the pack was finished. The court cards were splendid, in full colour: the kings with beards like mullahs, the queens in dresses with panniers, the jacks all as handsome as gods. As the game began, two women disturbed us. Actually, they took no notice of us but sat down facing each other and talked non-stop. From time to time they cast disapproving glances towards our den of vice. Eugenio squandered an entire packet of vanilla gums before he began winning. And the more I listened to the women, the more he won. Ear-catching sentences took my mind off the game. *He doesn't even know where I keep the washing powder.' 'You can imagine the state the house will be in when I get back.'* What was odd was the hint of triumph in the dry, slightly stale voice of the woman sitting beside me. She was quite pretty and also quite stupid. Blue eyes ringed with black lines, a tight little mouth, lipstick too pink.

'He doesn't even realize he's never there.'

'Even when he is there, he's never with us. In fact the children ignore him nowadays. A stranger.'

'Needs everything passed to him, over and over again, moans non-stop.'

'Droning on all the time, money worries, health worries.'

'I know! That everlasting egomania. Of course, the life he lives ...'

'Never says a word, the remote in one hand, snoring away.'

'Mine's going deaf, he's even given up squash.'

'Saturdays he has a snooze, never does anything with the kids. TV dinners suit him fine!'

It was a habit they had fallen into, these were like medicine balls they tossed back and forth, malicious gossip about husbands. A nasty habit. Cheap.

The words merged into a cloud, contaminating us. I wished we could close our ears. The game ended. Eugenio had cleaned me out. The train went through Landerneau, Landivisiau, the countryside sped by, army green, clumps of broom. Expecting that smell, nearly there now, my eyes strained for the sea.

'The first time you see it, make a wish,' I told Eugenio.

He shrugged: 'With you, it's making wishes all the time. They never work, anyway.'

'Oh no?' I retorted, taken aback. 'Give me a for instance.'

8

We arrived at Martha's place after dark. That was a disappoint-ment to me. I had been looking forward to showing my son its sovereign air, dominating the clifftop, an unforgettable memory, I hadn't been there for fifteen years but I instantly recognized the smell, the creaking, it all set up a strange feeling in me, a kind of joyous interest. Martha showed us upstairs, opened a door at the end of a passage. The room was smaller than I remembered, extremely plain, twin beds, small wooden table, two concrete shelves, painted green, washbasin, wardrobe; out-side the window a huge tree and, sensed beyond, the garden, frightening because of the darkness and the sound of the wind.

Martha said: 'Supper in an hour. Do you want to have a lie-down?'

As always in such circumstances, she addressed herself solely to me. Eugenio had often remarked on this:

'You'd think I was invisible!'

I told him it was her way of showing that she was a militant in the cause of protecting adults under threat from the civilization of the child as king. Eugenio's view was that I might have found him a different godmother.

'My godmother,' he used to say to anyone who would listen, 'is an enemy of children. She's against them, she hates them, and on top of that she's never given me a present. I don't know where mummy found her! What would you call someone who was the opposite of a gem?'

Martha's question sounded more like an order, so I said:

'Don't worry about us, see you in a while, everything's splendid. I love this room.'

That was not true at all, it had always scared me, it was the darkest room in the house, the only room without a sea view, and it was the one where you could hear the crows. I had bad memories of that room. But we were guests, extra guests, people they had taken pity on, Martha's mother had made that clear when she opened the door to us:

'Fifteen for Christmas, that's a first for this house. I don't know how we're going to cope, really I don't. There's already almost no coal left, and poor Catherine is going to have to sleep in the double bed with one of her daughters, having not got a wink of sleep last night because of Anne-Solange's triplets and their diarrhoea! She just takes it all, how many times have I told her: You'll be dead on your feet before they say thankyou, they won't lift a finger, for all that there are three of them, good evening, ma'am, good evening, sonny, anyway, Martha's in charge now, and since her father died the place has been a shambles!'

'That's enough, mum,' Martha said in that firm, humiliating tone that adults use with their parents when the roles have been reversed and everyone is engaged in the Grand Final Decline.

I said to Eugenio:

'Come on, I'll show you the beach!'

Before, I would never have dared leave our hosts like that, surely, it would have struck me as bad manners to dump our cases in the room and go straight out again, as if this had been a hotel. We live in a bad-mannered age, I thought, it would be presumptuous to imagine that none of it could possibly rub off.

I remembered the way to the beach. We crossed the garden, ignoring the strange-shaped shadows that fell across the path. I held Eugenio tightly by the hand as we ran down the muddy track leading to the inlet. The tide was in. We sat on a rock, looking at the lighthouse, the silvery sea, the moon, the vast, almost green sky, the glistening hulls of the pleasure-boats that spent the winter in the precarious shelter of the harbour. All around the bay, the little human lights of houses, cafés, cars, the streetlamps lining the sea road — all sparkled like wolves' eyes in the night. Two tuna boats were tied up at the jetty. Right at the end, I thought I could make out the entwined shapes of two lovers leaning against the beacon, but I couldn't have sworn to it, I tended to see lovers everywhere.

We sat there for some time, until our eyes hurt from peering into the twinkling darkness, the two of us hand in hand, teeth chattering quietly.

'I've never seen anything so marvellous, not ever,' my son said in an unsteady voice, and for a second I felt I had fulfilled my role on this earth.

In the drawing-room, everyone was busy studying photographs spread out on the floor.

'Catherine was clearing out the wash-house and she came across a suitcase full of photo albums, arranged by years. It's all here, everything!' Martha explained to me in a voice that shook with excitement.

She turned to Eugenio: 'Has your mother ever told you the story of our family?' And without waiting for a reply she started talking about splendid weddings, young men with chiselled features, the time when people knew how to receive at tea-time, the three hundred dresses her great-grandmother had owned, the baby lion that the Congolese ambassador had given Grandma for her seventh birthday, having heard that she was so bored there was a danger of her falling ill.

'Naturally, it was the baby lion that soon fell ill from being fed bottles of chocolate milk and forced to walk around in the clothes Grandma used to make for him, with little organdie caps on his head. They gave him to the zoo. I don't know what became of him, Grandma wouldn't talk about it. Possibly she missed the animal. We never did find out the lion's name. Even here, in the holiday house, which was called the "little house" as opposed to the two large town-houses that went to the cousins, there was a smoking-room, two reception rooms and two small studies. It was considered an absolutely indispensable mark of respect that everyone should have at least two rooms to retire to. Now they've all been turned into bedrooms or dormitories for the summer. As for Grandma, she died around the time of the fashionable soirées at the Grand Hotel. Just as well, really. She didn't see her world disappear. She never knew that young lads in shellsuits, with grubby faces and a marked propensity for giving the finger, had taken over the old clay courts in the grounds, ousting the elegant tennis-players of the Jazz Age.'

'I didn't realize you had this yearning for the past,' Martha's husband Étienne said acidly. 'I'll never understand how you and your family contrive to be so proud of your banker ancestors, your fallow fields, your wind-swept heaths, your amethyst quarries and your globe-trotting grandmothers. To be honest, I see only exploiters with an easy conscience, captains of industry taking a cheap pride in their pathetic veneer of culture, their three collectable paintings, their old books with the tattered bindings that nobody reads. Dubious women and capitalists in pigskin gloves, ill-concealed behind all their paternalistic talk. How can you swallow all that twaddle and still be openly left-wing, claiming to be a democrat and campaigning in the radical branch of the radiologists' union for the right to free false teeth for all?'

'Please, Étienne,' Martha's mother broke in. 'You are still in my house, so far as I am aware. Nor, unfortunately, am I completely deaf. Just keep these reflections of a jumped-up member of the lower-middle classes who fancies himself as a sociologist to yourself, and we'll all be the better for it. Good God, how I miss the days when parents arranged their children's marriages!' She had dropped stylishly into an armchair, fanning herself with a furry rabbit that she had just picked up.

'Nothing wrong with her!' I thought.

The double doors giving onto the terrace slammed, and everyone jumped.

'Ghost!' said Marie-Sandra with a screech of laughter.

The children had all disappeared. The four bigger girls had switched the television on and taken the triplets onto their knees. They were giving them a commentary on the latest game show. Seven girls, like in Grimms' fairy tales. Rather frightening, really.

'Dinner in ten minutes!' Martha shouted. She was sitting behind me. I picked up an album marked '1948-1949'. All the albums had two dates on the cover. I turned the pages with trepidation and also a certain emotion, although I hate photos. Photos are nearly always circumstantial evidence. Mendacious circumstantial evidence. Nothing ever happened the way the photos tell it, and yet, one day, what we remember is the photos, and nothing but the photos. Photos delineate a happy past, sun-drenched holidays, couples holding hands, lovers embracing in the intoxication of sensual pleasure, children running along beaches, shouting for joy. Photos are the lie that wins without a fight. A Stalinist invention. You never see photos of those deadly parties, those ghastly shopping-trips in icy supermarkets, stuffy dinners, arguments between brother and sister, irreparable disappointments, nascent divorces, ordinary boredom, rainy days. Photographers encourage us to yearn for a past that is not worth it. To weep for moments we were not enjoying and that never merited our tears. Hearing Martha, pink-cheeked with excitement, give a running commentary on the lives of her pale and legendary cousins in flowing dresses, white bloomers, boaters, their suitors in Panama hats and long shorts, I first put in some appropriate questions, inquiring after names. Then, bitten by goodness knows what Breton bug, perhaps carried away by the climate of controversy that seemed to reign in the house, I said:

'Photos make me think of that man armed with a Nikon who, on Beg-Meil beach last year, made his poor fiancée of a day pose like a mermaid at the water's edge, then in the water up to her waist, that arm a little higher, twist your hips, cup your breasts in your hands, now come out, sit down, be natural, more natural, sensual, more sensual, plunge your fingers into the sand. That was the point at which she rebelled. She couldn't abide sand, she was quite prepared to cater to the bloke's every whim, no problem, she thought it made a good picture, I don't know what she thought, probably nothing, or some notion of dream holidays, love, sex, but not including sand, sand was not modern, it stuck to your skin and made you itchy.'

Everyone was looking at me. Eugenio was studying his socks.

'Yes, well,' Marie-Sandra said, 'I seem to remember you being against everything.'

I imagined her, on a beach, posing for the camera.

'Not at all,' I stammered. 'I'm just saying.'

'Dinner's ready!' came Martha's shout from the kitchen. We all took our seats around the big family dining-table that filled one corner of the room. Someone removed the splendid bunch of holly from the middle and put it on the floor to make more space.

'I'll give it five minutes before someone knocks it over,' Étienne muttered, but he neither said nor did anything, which struck me as perverse or cowardly, I couldn't decide. What we had was a kind of female banquet, though that is a contra-diction in terms since nearly all the women were on their feet, as usual, half of them in the kitchen.

'As Yolande can't stay, we've planned dishes that will be easy to serve,' explained Anne-Solange, who had taken the seat beside me. 'Right, I'll sit here with you for a couple of minutes. Martha, Marie-Sandra, Catherine, that'll do in the kitchen.'

Unobtrusively, Anne-Solange was trying to make sure that she was boxed in.

Her three babies clung to her skirts, effectively anchoring

her. She did not even notice any more, she was so used to being a toboggan, crushed beneath the weight of Moira, Minna, and Melissa. Catherine came in carrying a salmon, Marie-Sandra brought a courgette gratin the size of a bicycle wheel and put it on the table, and Martha followed with slices of ham and a dish of pasta shells for the children.

Every day the same, day after day, how boring, I said to myself, suddenly sorry that I had accepted this invitation, worn out before I had done anything, worn out in advance by the washing-up, the shouting children, the next day's shopping, the other meals, countless meals, each more magnificent and perfect than the last.

Suddenly Martha's mother started talking fondly to me, fingering the top button of the orange blouse worn with a green cravat that had so impressed me on arrival.

'You have only the one child, my eldest daughter was telling me? I had four, four daughters, and seven granddaughters. I'd never have thought it would be the way it was, so much heartache, so many worries, and for what, one wonders in the end. My Henri died two years ago, cursing me because his name would die with him. No one knows what it's like, finding yourself on your own after fifty-two years of marriage. Oh, I've enough money, of course I have, the money came from my side of the family, that's why they never accepted Henri, nor, come to think of it, did I do much to defend him against all the humiliation. I would give anything, right down to my last teaspoon, to have him still.'

She had picked up my teaspoon and was trying to twist it in her blotched fingers.

'Hey, that's my spoon, Granny,' I pointed out, 'use your own!'

Some people's sacrificial outbursts need watching closely.

I noticed Eugenio looking at her in alarm.

'Salmon, mother,' Martha interrupted, filling her plate. 'You know you must eat. And leave poor Nouk alone. You're boring her to tears with your stories. Honestly, it's not done, talking about death during mealtimes.' I made a careful study of the swallows flying round my blue china plate.

Marie-Sandra gave a laugh:

'Papa had a list. We weren't allowed to talk about death, illness, anything to do with the body, that was vulgar, or to pass on tittle-tattle about anyone. No sex, of course, ever. No indiscretions, no religion, one didn't discuss famous people either, this wasn't a concierge's lodge. Gossip about Johnny Hallyday's latest fiancée had to be avoided, even harmless gossip. The economy was OK, so were topics of general interest, comments on social questions. Violence, pollution, state education, part-time work. Never speak well of your children, never speak ill of your colleagues: no one was interested. Oh, God!'

Catherine looked thoughtful.

'Nowadays, I've noticed, people talk mostly about what they've seen on television, which is a subject papa didn't get around to banning. He never even imagined its existence.'

The girls ate silently, at the two ends of the table, their expressions vacant.

'I think they've got lice, all four of them, I think their heads are crawling with lice,' Catherine said suddenly, after looking at them for a moment.

'My dear girl, you're mad!' exclaimed Martha's mother, abandoning the bit of salmon that she'd carefully mashed up, stirred around and mixed in with the bones and the gratin. 'We haven't seen lice since the war!'

'Anyway, if they have got lice, it's your daughters who passed them on to mine!' exclaimed Marie-Sandra. 'I shouldn't be surprised, either, considering where you live.'

There was not a scrap of salmon left, and Étienne was busy cleaning up the gratin dish. Moira, Minna, and Melissa, having spread a little more ham over their mother, had gone off in search of books for her to read to them. The big girls and Eugenio had vanished. The television could be heard.

'I have never seen children less willing to help nor so badly brought up,' the old lady muttered.

'Mother, please,' Marie-Sandra replied, enunciating crisply.

I wondered where all the husbands were.

After supper, the triplets took up a position under the tree and on top of their mother, busily sticking in needles all over her in an attempt to turn her into a tree as well.

'Anne-Solange is so patient!' her mother remarked. She had regained the patriarchal armchair and was once more fanning herself with the fluffy rabbit, this time because of the wine we had drunk with the meal.

Martha drew me into the kitchen to do the washing-up and answer my questions. We opened the window and sat on the sill for a smoke, like in the old days. Martha was still smoking untipped Pall Mall, cigarettes for the strong-minded, while I, with my 'light and mentholated' Peter Stuyvesant, felt distinctly uncool.

The waves were making an astonishing amount of noise.

'Spring tide!' Martha said with pride. The kind of pride that gave her a halo in the old days when she used to tell me about her sporting achievements, her rosettes for horse-riding, her Round the Bay Solo, her Twenty-Kilometre Skulls. What I secretly called her Nietzschean pride.

'Do you remember when we used to hunt squirrels?' That silenced us, it was such an old memory.

Stubbing out our butts in a dirty plate, we embarked on the big clean-up. Stacking the plates in order of size, rinsing the glasses, then the cutlery, drying-up systematically. Approached as a craft, washing-up is a noble and soothing activity, not unrelated to meditation.

'Where are all the husbands?' I finally asked.

'Mine is here, obviously. What about yours, where's he?' Martha snapped back, as if I had attacked her family.

'Your guess is as good as mine,' I replied sadly. 'It's been ages since I heard anything of Alfonso.' The first part was even truer than I thought, but I have often found myself saying things that meant more than I realized at the time.

Martha changed tack. As if her words had outstripped her thinking, or as if the points had been set wrongly somehow. She started telling me about Catherine, the extraordinary story of poor sad Catherine.

'Do you remember how we used to call her Saint Catherine? It made her cry. She used to say that, because of us, she'd never marry, but there was no chance of that: she was so pretty, the sweetest little mouse of all, Papa used to say. But she was also very serious. When she went to university to study law, she was surrounded by admirers, yet she never noticed a thing. She put a huge banner up in her room: "Women are waking up, who needs Prince Charming now?" She used to repeat that incessantly. But it was all she ever thought about, Prince Charming. Being worthy of him. She was convinced it was something you earned, like everything else. Hard, dedicated work. When she met Sacha, whose real name was Jean-Pierre or something perfectly ordinary like that, she decided he was the one. She —'

'Martha, you're boring me,' I said, breaking a glass by stuffing my damp teatowel into it too energetically. 'I know thousands of stories like this and I don't see what's special about Catherine's marriage. Your sister was always a bit of a pain in the neck, like all saints, and her husband eventually got fed up. A bloke calling himself Sacha, what do you expect?'

Martha gave me an intense look. She was going to make me listen, jolt me out of my rut, rip off my blinkers, imprison me in advance in her little private pillory. And I knew better than to venture too far into that kind of minefield.

'Imagine, she met her husband at a conference called "Capitalism: Its Promises and Disappointments in the Eastern Countries", and it was the start of a romantic idyll that lasted for years, love and political activism, a meeting of minds, love and friendship combined, cocking a snook at the cynics, the sermonizers, the killjoys. He was a brilliant public speaker, and what was more he adored her mind. He used to call her 'My Little Light' — Svetlana. The years passed, the girls grew up. Catherine lost her sparkle. In fact, she didn't shine at all any more. She'd become quite drab, glumly marking her pupils' homework, Year Ten economics and social sciences option, the emergence of currency, the domestic market, the return of Malthus, the crash of '29, two rivals: sugar beet and sugar cane, debt and its effect on household consumption, agricultural income and shagreen, the iron and steel industry as a thing of the past, the economy and conservation of the environment. All the questions that had once brought a gleam to her eye, for they heralded a new dawn, had become the bars of her cage, a routine without hope, lesson plans, no more than lesson plans, repetitive essays, pretexts for making spelling mistakes, uttering truisms, parroting catchphrases. So he did something about it, something special. He built her a study where she could work on her thesis, he told her. You must learn to assert yourself, darling, he said, then your hair will stop falling out all over the carpet, all over our pillows, all over my jacket, which I find particularly irritating, he added under his breath. You're much too wrapped up in me, the girls, your pupils. What's happened to the light in your eyes, the bloom in your cheeks? You must think of yourself from now on, he said, of your career. He made her a study in the basement. Apparently there was nowhere else for it to go. A glass-roofed study, for the light. When the cave of freedom was finished, you used to walk across Catherine's sky every time you entered their place. Very thick glass bricks, like you get in swimming-pools sometimes. Catherine joyfully took up residence in her coffin.'

'Snow White and her bier! You mean, sometimes Prince Charmings put their princesses back to sleep!' I said in the knowing voice of the attentive pupil. Martha's smile was unexpectedly severe.

'And then that bastard Jean-Pierre simply took off,' she said. 'Took off. Without leaving an address. "I couldn't help myself," he wrote in a note he left behind, "I have to save my skin." If you'd seen the state of his skin, but that's another story. On which note, my love, I must leave you for a moment, I need to make a phone call. I'm going to use the box down by the harbour. If anyone wants me, tell them I've gone for a walk.'

The washing-up was all put away, the kitchen sparkled. Martha makes me shiver, I thought, wondering why. I picked up a few more splinters of broken glass, then sat down again on the windowsill in the bizarre hope that an answer would emerge from the forest if I stared hard enough, emptying my mind. The crows cawed an accompaniment to the waves. I even heard an owl.

In the drawing-room, a game had been organized by Granny, Anne-Solange, Étienne and Aglaé.

'Come and sit down!' Étienne said, offering me a sheet of paper and a felt pen. 'You have to think of a definition of the word that Aglaé is going to tell us.

Aglaé, Marie-Sandra's eldest daughter, looked like a thin-lipped Queen of Sheba. Seated cross-legged on the divan, which was covered with Indian throws, she considered us. A dictionary lay open between her thighs.

'The word is *kartouli*,' she said. 'Everyone writes down a definition. I read them out. You have to guess which one comes from the dictionary and make the one you've invented sound convincing.'

Silence fell, for the space of about two minutes. Then Aglaé read out what we'd written, not a muscle of her face giving away what she felt.

'*Kartouli*, a kind of perfume from the Polynesian islands, *kartouli*, an African game like knucklebones, *kartouli*, a West Indian portolan, *kartouli*, a very old medical technique for treating rheumatic pains and cramps, *kartouli*, a Georgian dance performed like a love poem, following strict rules.'

A shout rang out.

It came from up above. The voice was Marie-Sandra's.

'It's nothing,' said Étienne, who had not moved. He looked at me sadly. 'Marie-Sandra loves a bit of drama.'

All the women had rushed to the bottom of the stairs. Marie-Sandra entered, holding a white hand-towel, which she pompously unfurled on the table.

The towel was covered with tiny black corpses, legs spread wide. Several hundred lice.

'It's Catherine. Look what she's just brought me. Perhaps now I'll believe my own eyes, she says. She's laid them all out carefully, look, she was working on it for some time, she and Sonia, in the bathroom. It's revolting. I'm not surprised Sacha dumped you, you poor cow.'

The work of art that Catherine and Sonia had created was in fact quite amusing. But modern art and fleas do tend to trigger unpredictable reactions. Marie-Sandra slumped against the big table, sobbing.

'Game's over,' Aglaé said. 'It was the Georgian dance performed like a love poem. Bedtime, I think, mummy,' and she put an arm around her mother's shoulders to lead her away. 'Come on, you're going to ring daddy and tell him all about it.'

I watched them leave the room; Aglaé and Marie-Sandra one way, Catherine and Sonia the other, two vestals and their mothers.

Martha was still not back from the phone box down by the harbour. How bold she is, I thought, with her rumpled hair like an adulteress. Like a free woman is what I actually thought, that's how much, without meaning to, we identify transgression with freedom. I thought, involuntarily, of Jason, the man who made love so marvellously, and Étienne, the archetypal tired-of-life man, and the ogre Sacha, and Henri, who had died. All those ghosts, what did they want with us, ultimately? And Pierre-Jean, we all called him *poor Pierre-Jean*, who had become Marie-Sandra's husband, to our huge surprise, and Alfonso, my own ghost, who had vanished so long ago I no longer wished to know why.

Quietly, I entered the crow room, our room.

On the double bed lay a small, prostrate body. Eugenio was crying. Had been for hours, possibly.

I shook him.

'Who hurt you, darling, who hurt you? What's going on? What happened to you?' I rubbed his back and fondled him, and not a sound came from him but the gulping of tears and the short swell of his sobbing.

'Eugenio, talk to me, please, talk to me.'

He said: 'I'm frightened, mummy. I don't like Martha, even if she is my godmother, even if she would always look after me, like you said. She's so sharp and hard, she's like a stone wall, and her mother's even worse.'

I was sure this was insufficient reason for crying like that. Crying like that, I knew, came from pain or grief. As if someone had just died, I thought. I told Eugenio: 'Sometimes, when someone dies, you don't feel like crying, even though you should, and the tears come later, without warning. When they do come, they hurt. They dig channels.'

'Sometimes, too, maybe, a person cries in advance,' was his comment. 'Also, you abandoned me. You didn't notice I'd gone. I told myself you'd come running, then I realized you'd forgotten all about me. Martha's family have taken you over.'

Eugenio was not crying any more. He talked in a lowered voice, his eyes were lowered too.

'You always let me down, mummy. It's like dad was saying on the phone, you're incapable of living a normal life with me. He said you'd gone a bit gaga, judging from rumours he'd picked up. He'd heard we were always on our own, just the two of us, he felt it was very dangerous, that sort of thing. All the experts on childcare and the family said so. He asked: "What do you think? Don't you agree, little chap?" That's what he told me. Is it true, mummy? I heard them all talking on the telephone, Martha was there. They said you were so fragile, too much of a risk, for yourself and probably also for a child, with your cast of mind, your heredity, your mental heredity. They talked about an "unreality gene". I've got all the words in my head now, I can't get rid of them.'

I looked at Eugenio in disbelief. Outside, gulls began screaming in the darkness.

9

I felt cold all of a sudden. There was a smell of decay in the room. A wave of loneliness swamped me.

'You couldn't turn the light on, could you, mummy?' Eugenio asked.

He had dried his eyes and was sitting up on the bed, knees drawn up, back against a floppy white pillow that protected him from the roughcast wall. I often used to wonder, who invented roughcast? Some mad, dangerous sadist, no doubt, a disciple of Schopenhauer's hedgehogs who apparently complained of cold as they moved away from the fire and tore one another to bits as they approached. The two green wrought-iron lamps bent their spindly necks towards us, and I climbed on the bed to sit in symmetry with my son, with my knees drawn up and my eyes fixed on the giant shadows thrown by the petals of the dried hydrangeas. Huge blue blooms impregnated with slate-grey, everlasting, like dull, indifferent angels, they were the only ornament in the room.

I also turned on the radio, to drive away the ghosts.

On the radio, people always sound happy and fearless. They discuss things. Sometimes they get the giggles, when one of them makes a Freudian slip or gives a silly answer. Nothing is ever solemn, because there are no pictures. Consequently, they can be serious if the fancy takes them. You see neither the rings under their eyes, nor their agonized looks, nor how they have aged. Eternity is on their side, and they toss ideas back and forth as if playing ball. Ideas are the best weapon I know against a bad mood. Two or three lively voices talking about something or other, it's a kind of game, trying to identify the subject, perhaps guess what is hidden behind the words they reel off, the topic under discussion. Sheer curiosity forces you out of yourself.

A number of voices, which I made no attempt to distinguish, were recalling writers, artists, anyway people who had been immortalized by Truman Capote and the photographer Richard Avedon. Quite soon, the conversation took off:

'These are secular saints, each tortured by an obsession — and as Gauguin said, I paint transience — inhabited by the dilemma of being human. Gauguin, really? Well, if you must use the word "obsession" for the most elementary requirements — growing old, living, or pausing to capture beauty. What was it Guy Debord used to say? Cut the twaddle, was that it? Please, do let's stop exploiting the dead like this! (General hubbub.) Or else sacrifice everything to the moment, snow, Rilke, or a swan, can we still see? Lies, lies, and more lies! A novel, surely, is first and foremost a way of seeing? Couldn't the same be said of advertising? You jest, my friend? The painter, woman, poet, child, oh blessed squaring of the circle of the pieties incessantly rising from their ashes! If we but knew a fraction of what the powers that be conceal from us nowadays, murderers,

we're at the mercy of murderers, Rimbaud said, devil take your reeking dimples! Paranoia has ceased to be critical, there's the rub! Is there not more poetry in a child than in all the alexandrines of all the official poets of all time? (Laughter, clink of glasses, sound of ashtrays being used.) And do you believe that a person who does not feel constrained to create can be a true creator? Go back to Madame de Sevigny, nothing is worth being for its own sake. What do we know of beauty? That it is tragic? (Laughter.) Think of Karen Blixen's face, her dark eyes. No one ever chooses pain. Let him who professes poetry know that he will never attain it. (Laughter, sound of joints cracking, jaws, tinkle of glasses.) How Jansenist can you get, my friend? The natural, it's so easy to say, four hours a day at my desk, otherwise I suffer from headaches and can't stop writing, to me that's the sign of the artist. True morality has no time for morals. And if one quite simply never had to ask oneself the question. . . And for the labourer, the solid godliness of honest toil, performed for its own sake, which in this day and age is virtually impossible, admit it, those who say otherwise are liars, writers have to look like actors, imagine all the care that takes, particularly for women, even bishops, cardinals, and popes are performers. Go back to your little stone seat in the forest, friend!'

'Can you turn it off, mummy? Or find Fun Radio?'

I had already explained to Eugenio that I could not stand listening to Fun Radio. Certainly not with him. I found it offensive. 'It's a question of generation,' Nicole had once told me, she kept a file on adolescents and the culture of sex on the radio. 'You're not hearing the same thing as them. You make a drama out of what they just find amusing. You take it seriously. To them it's a game.'

To Nicole, everything was a question of generation. The

concept had conveniently replaced ideology, the class struggle, feminism, psychoanalysis, minority cultures, all her previous grids for interpreting the world. I allowed my mind to wander. I found comfort in thinking about Nicole and hence about the office, my nest, my anchor, my security, possibly the one place on earth where I was expected and where I had my own chair, for ever. Civil servant, it sounded solid, four-square. Every day the same, over and over. I drifted off, far from the fetid swamp I had committed us to in my belief that I was doing the right thing. Holidays, family, what a rip-off.

But here was Eugenio, suddenly bright as a button, itching for an argument: 'Well, I do find Fun Radio amusing. All my friends listen, we swap stories. Some incredibly funny people ring in, plus you learn lots of things, and the people are really nice. And funny. They try to help people. More than your dusty old fuddy-duddies who only say things no one understands. They do it deliberately, or maybe they're born like it, maybe they have this unreality gene too?'

I was angry now.

'Yes, they do,' I said composedly, 'all men and all women do, if you think about it. It's like madness and loneliness, my love, it's for everyone, but most people don't want to know that because they're afraid or because they don't have the means either to bear them or to understand them. So they become spiteful and violent, their lives turn sour. In the end they die, clawing their beds in fury.'

Eugenio was drawing threads from the white cotton bedspread and weaving them into a little plait. A blue-grey hydrangea petal twirled down and fell in front of us, like a comma.

'All we'd need is two radios and two headsets,' he suggested, dreamy-eyed. 'What's that noise? Sounds like a helicopter landing on the lawn.'

I looked out of the window, opening it wide. A lungful of cold, salty breeze took me by surprise. There was no one out there. In the distance, boats rocked, as far as the eye could see. I could hear their creaking.

'Time to go to sleep, darling.'

'I just know I'm going to have nightmares.'

He threw me a devilish, intimate, fond look.

'You could read to me or you could make up a story like when I was small. That'll keep the ghosts at bay, you always used to tell me.'

'You could read by yourself for a bit,' I said with dignity.

'No, because I don't like reading, and it's because of you.'

I felt myself go pale. I shrank from demanding an explanation.

'Everything's always because of me, everyone knows that. It's not an explanation, it's a simple tautology.'

'You shouldn't use words I don't understand,' Eugenio said. 'Martha said so. The thing with books, because you used to read to me too much when I was little, I can't get *weaned*. It's no good just being able to read. You forgot to make me want to *strive for independence*. I read too much in the womb.'

'Oh I see,' I said, too curtly, 'and do you have any other stupid theories to offer? Anyway, who gave you this neat explanation about weaning and striving?'

I knew perfectly well it was Martha again.

'Martha did.'

'Martha doesn't know anything about it. She's a dentist.'

'She's studied psychology too, and dad says she's a very sensible person.'

'She's never had children,' I said, mortified. 'How dare she play the expert?'

'Dad says she decided not to have children because she knows how much harm mothers do in this world. He says it's a mark of deep wisdom.'

'Quite true!' I said, planting a kiss on his eyes. I remembered: that was how we had become friends, Martha and I, all those years ago. We had taken turns at cursing our mothers while drinking mint syrup on a sunny terrace near the school. I even remembered the smell of the lilacs. Mothers! we moaned. Was not literature full of their crimes, their moral complacency, their complaints, their ravages? Count us out! we chorused. Never again, and never us!

Martha had kept her word, I reflected. Yet there she was, surrounded by her family, a kind of premature patriarch, and there was I with her, no man to hold me in his arms at night but, curiously, accompanied by a small boy; not at all what we had dreamed of. There we were, I thought with a smile, nearing the end of December, in those dreadful last few days of the year, and Martha had her mother beside her, and I knew it was soothing me, this brief plunge into a past now gone for ever. How odd, I mused, that memories mellow us when they should make us weep.

'I'll tell you the story of *The Four Principles of the Perfect Woman*,' I announced to my son. 'A Fulani story, both beautiful and profound.'

'Oh no, not that one! You always tell that one. It's a girl's story. I hate it when there are fairies. I want *Half Chick*.'

Eugenio had slipped between the sheets and curled up in a ball. I straightened the collar of his pyjamas, which were printed in the colours of some basketball club, cows' heads that have some sacred meaning for him.

And I told him the story of *Half Chick*, who was so cunning he had lent the king a hundred crowns and so strong he could carry all his friends on his neck. 'Come, little fox, hop on my neck,' was one of Eugenio's favourite sentences, along with 'River, river, leave me be, or this little chick is lost!'

When Half Chick was made king, and the people acclaimed him, delighted to have a monarch who was so good at business as well as making friends, Eugenio fell asleep holding my hand.

It took me a while to unfasten his fingers. The river of Lethe ran between us. Even though I had stayed with my child to the end, keeping my darling's fears at bay, as our fingers parted I felt the separation.

I heard sounds in the garden, some sort of procession. From the window I saw Martha and her sisters. They were wearing hoods, carrying torches. That dull sound was still there. A motor of some kind, thrumming and causing the house to vibrate.

I went out and joined them. The grass was damp and came straight through my thin shoes.

'I thought you'd gone to bed,' Martha said, squeezing my arm. She used the strange, sickly-sweet tone of voice I had first heard her use one day when she rang me, an actressy voice, very solemn and modulated, it made me want to laugh. 'We decided to visit Papa's grave. Come along if you like, he was fond of you.'

That bit was absurd, but I went with them. A band of Inquisition penitents, a Ku Klux Klan posse, Carnival at Christmas time, I could feel a cold coming on.

'I put the machine on after supper, the washing piles up so quickly, and nothing dries here!' Anne-Solange murmured. 'I hope it didn't stop your son going to sleep?'

'So that was the helicopter full of Martians!' I said, shivering. She gave me a bewildered look.

Henri's grave was at the bottom of the garden, just beyond the washing lines. It stood on a patch of grass above the sea, surrounded by a ring of brambles. Mulberries provided shade in summer. Henri rested there alone, with no stone, only a cross, some low-growing flowers and a few shells half-hidden in the grass, votive offerings from the granddaughters. I liked him being there, close to the smell of washing, visited regularly. Marie-Sandra went every day. She had been his favourite, his darling little one. I knew she had frequently interrupted his studies to keep him company, at a time when his wife had other interests, apparently. Because Granny, like her eldest daughter, was one of those Amazons that have always been around, simultaneously reassuring and terrifying, implacable foster mothers, indefatigable matrons, husband-slayers, with God on their side, as Bob Dylan sings, adept at dedicating their daughters to the cult of father-worship. Clytemnestras.

That evening, however, at that late hour, Granny was asleep, lying on her back in a dignified pose, head carefully propped in the centre of her huge pillow, ready to be found dead in the morning, as she always used to say.

'It's a discipline,' she said, 'the hardest of all, keeping one's sleep. It's a question of faith.'

It was her proudest boast: still, at her age, falling asleep in five minutes, like a baby, after first praying for her loved ones.

And over the invisible grave the daughters were each silent

for a moment, keeping their father up to date with everything. They used to say he gave them advice and guidance. Martha had a wealth of examples of decisions she would never have taken without him.

The sea roared, clouds scudded across the moon, out on the water the shrouds moaned.

Abruptly, everyone got up, the ceremony was over. My teeth were chattering. The need to believe, so typical of the nineties, takes some painful forms.

'He said he was glad you were here,' Martha said softly to me in her special voice, slipping her arm beneath mine. I checked an impulse to shrug.

There was something magical about the lights of the drawing-room sparkling through the two glass doors. How Hansel and Gretel watch over our dreams, I thought. From far off we could see the table, the chairs, the panelled walls, like a promise of comfort. A world enclosed, protected, a nest. Bird-catchers' twaddle: there are no nests.

'Who'd like some ice cream?' cried Marie-Sandra. She made up dishes of vanilla ice cream. We installed ourselves in the kitchen like naughty children. The table was covered with jars of strawberry jam and rhubarb preserve, cold meats and pâtés, blackcurrant liqueur, crumbly cake, cognac and cheeses like little white pies. We were young girls again, with appetites like horses. Martha performed volubly, charmingly. We ate with our fingers, talked noisily and drank straight from the bottle.

The vanilla ice cream looked lovely, with its egg-yellow colour and the little black seeds dotting it, but it tasted like rancid butter. Martha's sisters laughed out loud. I chose to remain silent, wrapped in warm feelings, exuberance, even joy. At the same time I felt useless and fragile: a weed amid a riot of bloom. Ingratitude, I find, is always poised to spring.

In minutes the table was transformed into a wasteland, our savagery inscribed in every scrap of debris littering its wooden surface. Greasy crumbs were embedded in the very grain of the oak.

'Jacqueline's been a new woman since her mother died!' Marie-Sandra remarked, helping herself to more rabbit pâté. 'It's nearly always the way in the end.'

Confusedly, my mind tried to follow her into her world of psychological fiction, a world governed by the simplified rules of unresolved Oedipal conflicts in late twentieth-century woman. With a hint of that comical jealousy we feel towards people who inhabit our loved ones' minds but whom we do not know, I asked who Jacqueline was.

Martha roared with laughter.

'One of our pet projects: a poor little anorexic of thirty-five who sometimes looks fifteen and sometimes fifty, highly intelligent, teaches Greek at university. She walked into Marie-Sandra's beauty salon one day four or five years ago. No idea what had driven her to it, because she wouldn't let anyone touch her. They can be as bright as you like, it's as if they can't see the problem! A lack of common sense verging on idiocy. She was in a dreadful state, skin totally dehydrated, decalcified, dephos-phated, you can't imagine. I took care of her teeth for free, virtually. She needed a whole new mouth. She'd worn the ivory off her incisors, destroyed her molars. Such a lovely jaw originally! But the one we've remade is even better, I reckon. Marie-Sandra persuaded her to have a few collagen injections because of her premature wrinkles, and she took up swimming. With her mother dead, you'll see: the sky's the limit.'

Anne-Solange, who does not usually say much, offered in a slightly saucy voice:

'All she needs now is a boyfriend!'

Marie-Sandra modestly lowered her eyes to the piece of bread she had just spread.

'It's true, Jacqueline is a real success story. I'm pleased.'

'Do you get many patients like that?' I said, my interest aroused, my heart fluttering slightly.

Screaming was heard. Moira, Minna, and Melissa had woken up.

Anne-Solange and Catherine ran from the room. It was nearly two in the morning.

Martha turned to me: 'Come and help me empty the washing-machine,' she suggested in her angelic voice. 'That'll make Anne-Solange happy.'

'Right,' I said, puzzled. 'As if we were the shoemaker's little elves, who did his work during the night, do you remember, and in the morning he woke up all amazed.'

I was not sure I had the energy to be an elf. The throbbing of the helicopter had stopped. No doubt that was what had woken the babies.

The laundry was a former bathroom, now disused, filled with washtubs, half-empty packets of detergent, plastic watering-cans of all sizes and colours, filthy rags, wicker baskets filled with permanently damp floorcloths, two overflowing bags of washing, all of it sandy and sticky. Martha opened the window of the washing-machine for me and I found myself on all fours, livid but impotent, pulling out cotton nappies, nylon panties, rayon blouses, sleepsuits and astronomical numbers of socks.

It all smelled horribly of vomit. I was not sure whether that came from my muddled wits, the machine, the walls, or what.

'There's a funny smell,' I said cautiously to Martha. 'Maybe the sleepsuits need doing again.'

'Don't worry, it's always like that. It's the room that smells. The smell doesn't stay on the clothes, it disappears as they dry. It's always been like that. The laundry smells of sick, and the car smells of cat's pee. There's nothing anyone can do. Just not be too sensitive, that's all.'

She gave me a kiss, took me in her arms. I noticed the wrinkles on her neck.

'We haven't had time to talk. But I've been thinking a lot about you lately. Eugenio is ruining your life. And you are damaging him.' Martha's voice had gone actressy. 'Look at your wrists, I could break them with my little finger. I saw what was going on when you told me you never wanted to touch a paintbrush again, you'd lost faith in your talent, it was all nonsense, too tiring. I saw that what I'd taken for a long time to be a break, probably a necessary break after your too-sudden success, was something more serious, something unacceptable. I knew I had to do something. You've changed so much. Your son is such a problem, and you're so fragile.'

I wanted to wash my hands, I had this lingering smell of vomit on them, this fetid smell. Like a nagging symptom of something I wished to hide.

10

Next morning Eugenio was not in his bed and the house was silent.

It was a fine day, and I was by myself. There was a note on the kitchen table: 'See you soon. Signed: Everybody.'

I strolled down to the harbour for a coffee. The road smelled good, every pebble reminded me of something. I felt light at heart. Sun, coffee, a newspaper. I allowed my mind to roam, watched the passers-by, watched the tuna boats unloading their salted cargo out at the end of the jetty, listened to my neighbours, not for any reason, just for a laugh. I lit a cigarette.

I savoured my happiness, a woman on her own, a smile on her lips, at peace, mind as clear as the sky. This was me, strong and at peace. Free, free, free. I opened the newspaper. There was a double-page spread on the British queen. The need to modernize the monarchy or something. I cut it out for Eugenio.

'Look at Charles!'

I gave a start. Little Charles (nothing to do with the poor prince) was a stupid-looking little pooch with floppy ears. He was zigzagging between the tables, grunting like a pit bull terrier.

'He's the image of his father physically, but spiritually he's all me!' said a well-wrapped fat lady.

And I woke up completely.

Full of enthusiasm, I thought of the day ahead. I resolved to devote more time to Eugenio. We could go out on the rocks beyond the sea wall at low tide, I thought. There are crabs, I'll show him how to catch them, maybe we'll find other creatures.

What I should like to do, I decided, was to assemble the sort of collage picture we used to make as children; a sea hoard, we called it. We had taken the idea from a Prévert poem: 'To Make a Portrait of a Bird'. We collected crabs of various sizes, dead ones, then we dried them. Next, we painted them like masks, landscapes, geometrical figures, faces too. There also had to be a background: on a huge sheet of paper, sometimes on a real canvas or on a sheet of plasterboard, we glued real seaweed, painted shells, little stones. Finally, we added the crabs and starfish.

Eugenio would be sure to like that, I felt. It was quite like the maze in the carpet, what I called our Songlines. I should have to explain to Martha that this was how my passion for painting had become transmuted. That she must stop pining for the old days, my shows, the parties she used to throw for me, the career brought down in full flight. I remembered her stern warning: 'Listen to me, Nouk, otherwise I shall have to do something drastic. Listen to me, you simply do not have the right.'

But what is the point of art, I had wanted to say, if it is not life, if it steals life and gives nothing back? My hopes, once dead twigs, burst into leaf. A different kind of painting, truer, simpler, without fancy brushwork, modest, craft-based, coming from the heart and capable of changing the way we see the most ordinary things, the most anonymous people, telling it the way it is.

Suddenly, words sickened me. My eyes sought the sea.

In the distance I spotted the telephone box, a small lunar oblong at the end of the quay. Inside it, Martha telephoning. My heart stood still. As if her madness threatened me, I administered a stern 'Mind your own business'. Suddenly, the coffee tasted funny. I felt stifled. The sky was almost black.

I ran off, hoping she hadn't seen me.

At the end of the mole, out by the lighthouse, a man and a child were walking. I saw them through a blur, because of the drizzle that had begun to fall, because of the low cloud. The man and the small boy descended the steps to the little beach and walked towards the edge of the sea. They were holding hands. Then they were running, the man swung the boy up on his shoulders, spun him round, dropped him back on the sand. I could hear their distant laughter. They were playing.

Men and boys. There are moments, I told myself, where women have no place, moments that elude us and that I knew, for certain, I should never experience.

A sense of lightness.

I began walking towards them.

I went down the steps to the beach. Suddenly, I realized that the two were Eugenio and his father. I saw that they were Eugenio and his father. They could not see me.

I approached them and said: 'Shall we go and look at the tuna boat, then?'

'You might say hello,' said the man I no longer knew, and I said hello since there was no reason not to.

The sailors on the tuna boat were friendly. They invited us aboard. The hold was red with rust, the smells overpowering. Eugenio ran about, snooping in every corner. We heard shouting. On an upper deck he had found a tank full of giant turtles. His shouts had woken them, and they were climbing up on one another's backs to see what was happening. One of the sailors joined us. He caught one of the turtles in a net and turned it over. Its ventral carapace, white like an angel's breastplate, was tattooed all over with pen drawings, superb hieroglyphics, Chinese ideograms.

'This one could be a thousand years old,' the man said. 'I never show them to people. The little boy needed to see one, that's why I'm giving him this memory. The turtle says: "You owe no one. Launch out, don't ever be afraid."' He caressed the white belly, put his lips to a particular tattoo, righted the animal, returned it to the tank.

'*Ciao*, my beauty. Do you like birds, son?'

Eugenio did not answer. He just gazed at the man.

The sailor disappeared through a doorway and came back with a little cage shaped like a temple.

'Nightingales,' he said. 'You know, like the Chinese emperors used to have. Only these two haven't been blinded, but they sing anyway.' He thought about this. 'Maybe they sing a little less well, who knows?'

'The British queen collects birds, too,' Eugenio said then, proudly. 'Including nightingales, I saw them on television, the same, hundreds of them. It's like her picture collection, draw-ings by Leonardo da Vinci, Virgins with Child, studies of rabbits, princesses in dresses of scratchy fabric, St. Annes, angels, skeletons, men's legs, strange machines, sparrows, several Stabat Mater Dolorosas. At least six hundred pictures altogether. She's got everything in her castles, thousands of etchings, wood-cuts ...'

'Museum painting doesn't interest me,' the sailor said. 'Sorry. And the queen, quite honestly, makes me sick. I have my reasons, they're my business and no one else's. Here, take the nightingales, sonny, they'll teach you a few tricks and they're for you.'

He escorted us to the gangway. We walked back up to the house, Eugenio carrying his cage.

Martha immediately took me aside, into the kitchen. She was wearing her great-occasion manner.

'I didn't think it was going to happen like that!' she said. 'Your husband was supposed to arrive for lunch. As a surprise for you. You've not seen each other for so long. I think he was missing his son too badly, he's got married again, did you know, to a brilliant young psychiatrist. He wants to give your little boy a proper home. When he came to me to talk about it, I thought: What a splendid solution for everyone! Also, when he explained things to Eugenio I thought he was terrific, so sensitive, so perceptive. He told him: "You can choose, Eugenio. It's your choice." Eugenio immediately started talking about you. He said: "What about mummy, what does she think?" And we explained that you'd given up so many things for him. That you were a fragile soul and needed to paint to maintain your equilibrium. He said he thought so too. And anyway, a boy that age needs male company. You know what becomes of them when we cling too much. You wouldn't want your son to grow up a drag queen, would you? The Greeks and Romans used to take boys away from their mothers as soon as they turned seven.'

'And what good did that do?' I said. 'They had no drag queens, I suppose, your Greeks and Romans?'

I was quite simply stunned. Martha had always professed boundless admiration for homosexuals, their courage, their power of subversion. 'All the great writers,' she used to say. 'Painters. Art.'

Never for one moment had I imagined that she did not believe what she was saying. That she was on the side of the family, of normal people. That she fancied she knew anything at all about what makes people the way they are.

That she could ever have such power over my life. Or be in a position to wield it.

I looked at her in disgust.

'How can you have the faintest idea what will become of my son? What has it got to do with you, anyway? You don't even like him.'

Mentally, Martha was on her high horse. She looked down at me scornfully, nudging me with her lance.

'And his father? Do you know how much his father has suffered?'

'No, I do not. How can anyone know such things?'

The image of Eugenio on his father's shoulders clouded my vision.

Something had happened. Had maybe already happened a hundred times. Or ten thousand.

Something that must be accepted without the slightest protest, without making a fuss, without disturbing anything whatsoever. Leaving everything intact. For later.

Beside the drawing-room fire, Eugenio and his father were watching the nightingales.

In the real world, I told myself, sorrow springs from joy, and the end product is mortal fear. What would become of the apartment, I wondered, the little green plaque, Adam, the path scissored in our fitted carpet, our puzzles, the red curtain? Gone for ever.

I had no idea what I was going to do. Sometimes one cannot see so much as one step ahead.

There was no road map any more, no road, even. Nothing at all.

I wandered down to the beach, taking the old path. I walked towards the water, my pockets full of pebbles. Who was it talked about pockets full of pebbles? Oh how stupid they are, those stories, nothing ever happens, nothing special, really it doesn't. The water had never looked so grey.

No one, I thought, could ever paint a grey like that.